The Cooler

George Markstein was a military correspondent with the US Forces in Europe after World War II and has been hooked on the study of espionage ever since. He turned from documentary writing for television to drama, created the controversial 'The Prisoner' series, and has edited 'Danger Man', 'Callan' and 'Armchair Theatre'. He was co-winner of the British Writers Guild award for the Best Original Screenplay for the feature film *Robbery* in 1967, and is at present Executive Story Editor for Thames Television.

George Markstein

The cooler

Pan Books
London and Sydney

First published 1974 by Souvenir Press Ltd
and simultaneously in Canada by J. M. Dent & Sons (Canada) Ltd
This edition published 1975 by Pan Books Ltd,
Cavaye Place, London SW10 9PG
2nd printing 1975

ISBN 0 330 24295 4

Printed in Great Britain by
Richard Clay (The Chaucer Press) Ltd, Bungay, Suffolk

This story is fiction.
But there was a Cooler.
Those who know about it don't have to be told any more.
Those who don't can't be told any more.

Abbreviations

ISRB	Inter Services Research Bureau
SOE	Special Operations Executive
SPOC	Special Projects Operation Centre
SIB	Special Investigation Branch
STS	Special Training Schools

TOP SECRET

For CAPTAIN JAMES LOACH
Operation Instruction F486

Operation JESTER

Field Name PIERRE

Name on papers RAOUL DUBOIS

1 You will return to France, to continue with the duties assigned to you within the mission of your circuit.
2 You will proceed to France by bomber or Lysander to a point to be specified on your departure.
3 You will be received by a reception committee, who will give you any assistance you may require during the first few hours after your arrival and will see you on to a train to get to your final destination. Alternatively, they may give you instructions to proceed by road. After leaving the reception committee, you will break all contact with them.
4 You have been given a cover story and papers in the name of Raoul Dubois, which you will use for your normal life in the field. If you must assume a new identity in the field, you will inform us immediately. Your identity as an agent is covered by the name PIERRE.
5 You will work closely with SIMONE, who is to act as your radio operator. She will be under your command, but it must be understood that she is the ultimate judge in all questions of communications and wireless security. She will encode the messages herself.
6 You will take with you to the field the sum of 500,000 francs. You will give us an idea as early as possible of what your financial needs are likely to be.
7 You will send us as soon as possible the address of a postbox through which we can contact you in the event of radio communications breaking down.

8 You will be constantly working under conditions of maximum security.
9 Your courier will be MARCEL.
10 You have been given verbal instructions about the alternatives open to you in the event of capture.
11 You have been fully briefed about the system of BBC messages which will be used to transmit special orders.
12 You will renew such contacts as you made on your previous missions, but it is left to your discretion whom you trust.
13 In the event of any suspicion of security risk, you will take no chance but act in the surest way to eliminate that risk.
14 You will destroy these instructions prior to departure in the presence of Major Ince.

Loach

I

Loach was awake for several moments before he opened his eyes.

He had slept well, but the bed was unfamiliar. His eyes still closed, he listened to the distant noise of traffic. Gradually, he relaxed.

It was all right. He was still in London. No need to be tense – yet. No pistol under the pillow. Not till tomorrow.

He lit a cigarette. This was a moment to savour. The next few hours were his own, before he reported to them.

After that...

1500 hours, they had said. Seven hours to go.

Loach got out of bed, and shuffled over to the window in his bare feet. He peered out. The mews was empty except for a man fiddling with a car in front of the small garage.

Loach enjoyed not having to study the man. This time tomorrow, a stranger across the way meant danger. A man casually fixing a car engine might be the first hint of the end.

But not today.

Loach went into the small kitchen, and started to make himself a cup of tea. It was all there, kettle, milk, tea caddy, sugar.

The flat was cosy, and beautifully kept. It wasn't the first time that Loach had stayed in one of their safe apartments, but he had never seen a cleaning woman, or anybody who collected the rubbish, or delivered the milk. The places were always spotless, but the people who looked after them seemed to be invisible.

Idly, Loach wondered what sort of cleaning woman the organization would employ anyway. Some Cockney lady maybe, who took a pride in her unknown gentlemen?

Gentlemen who would often never come back for a second stay. Because they were dead.

The kettle whistled, and Loach made his tea. Two lumps, just a dash of milk.

That's a thought, he mused. Who else had they put into this neat little apartment behind the Albert Hall? Viner, just before he was captured and shot? Etienne, on the eve of the mission from which he never returned?

Loach decided they had a surprise coming. He was coming back.

He dressed carefully. At first he was going to put on his captain's uniform. Then he saw the grey suit in the wardrobe. Why not? He hadn't worn it much anyway, and he wouldn't have to give any salutes.

The newspaper lay on the mat, neatly folded. Again, he hadn't heard anyone push it through the door. They probably had their own phantom newsagent, like the charlady and the milkman.

The front page wasn't very exciting, and anyway he had heard most of it on the nine o'clock news last night. The Russians had crossed some unpronounceable river in the Ukraine, American bombers had raided Berlin again, the British were advancing in Burma, and King Peter of Yugoslavia had arrived in London.

Outside, the weather was beautiful, clear skies, and a lot of sunshine. Loach decided he might take a stroll through the park.

Then the phone rang.

Loach picked it up warily.

'Yes?' he said. No number, no name.

'Captain Loach?' said the prim voice.

She didn't have to say any more.

'Yes,' said Loach. He knew who it was.

'Could you pop round and see Major Ince?' she said. But it wasn't really a question.

'I'm due there this afternoon,' said Loach. '1500 hours.'

'No, could you come now,' she said. 'Say in half an hour?'

'All right. Half an hour.'

Loach slammed the phone down.

He felt like kicking their tasteful bloody furniture. It's all right for them, sitting in their offices around Baker Street, shuffling memos and reports, hiding maps behind little curtains, and sounding mysterious. He only had seven hours left.

Loach locked the front door of the mews flat, and looked for a taxi. Then he thought again. To hell with it, I'll walk through the park. So I'll be there in forty-five minutes. They can damn well wait.

At the Albert Memorial, Loach allowed himself a smile. He almost hoped he'd be late. It would annoy Ince, tidy, precise, correct Major Ince. Ince might even look up and say stiffly, 'Loach, you're late. I asked you to be here in half an hour.'

And Loach would relish telling him, 'Too bad, you little twot. Now you can fire me.'

That would be something, F Section kicking out an agent because he was twenty minutes late.

Loach enjoyed the walk, right across the park at a fast, brisk pace. Again the wonderful, free feeling of not having to bother about anyone. Not the man reading the newspaper on the park bench, not the two men strolling behind him.

This time tomorrow, of course...

Near the anti-aircraft battery at Marble Arch, Loach saw a girl walking a dog. He didn't really look at her face, but he took in her body, her legs. He was irritated at having spent last night like a monk, all tucked up in the flat in solitude. His last night too. He could have done with that girl in bed beside him.

It was only that after the briefing they gave him yesterday, he had too much on his mind.

'Excuse me, sir,' said the American.

Loach stared at him. He was a sergeant in the Army Air Corps, with 8th Air Force shoulder patches. For a second, alarm, almost panic flooded over Loach. And as quickly, common sense took over again, told him to relax.

'Yes?' said Loach.

'Sir, can you direct me to the Washington Club,' said the over-polite, over-correct American. 'On Curzon Street.'

'Curzon Street,' repeated Loach. 'Yes. Go down Park Lane – then ask at the Dorchester. They'll tell you.'

'Thank *you*, sir,' said the polite American.

Loach looked after him. Is that bastard trying to send me up? Suddenly he didn't feel like walking any more.

He hailed a cab.

'Paddington Street,' he told the driver. 'Just off Baker Street.'

2

Loach paid off the cab at the flower shop, and then walked round the corner. He never understood the point of the small black metal plaque outside the house – 'Inter Services Research Bureau'.

Ince smiled his cold smile, and told him to sit down.

'Beautiful weather,' said Ince.

If you were a bank manager, you'd now produce a glass of sherry, thought Loach.

Aloud, he said, 'Yes, should be all right tonight.'

Ince brushed some non-existent crumb from his bare desk.

'It's about tonight,' he said. 'Cigarette?'

He produced a packet, and Loach took one. It was Loach who lit them both.

'Thank you,' said Ince. Then, almost in the same breath: 'I'm afraid tonight is off.'

Loach stared at him.

'Confounded nuisance for you, I know,' said Ince, without a trace of sympathy. 'But we've had to scrub it.'

'When do I go?' asked Loach.

'Soon,' said Ince.

Loach felt a tightening of his stomach muscles. Something was wrong, desperately wrong.

'What's happened?'

'We'll have to change a few things,' said Ince.

Loach felt like shaking him.

'Why? Everything's all set.'

'Was all set,' said Ince. 'Now we have a problem.'

He opened a drawer in his desk, took out a file with the big red X on it. Loach knew those files were always kept under lock and key – so Ince had stage-managed this, put the Top Secret folder in his desk to produce it on cue.

'It's Jester, I'm afraid,' said Ince.

'Go on,' said Loach, tersely.

'The circuit's been – destroyed. I'm afraid Jester's had it.'

'The whole circuit?' said Loach. 'Between yesterday and this morning? I don't believe it.'

Ince opened the file, took out the pink priority message slip, and handed it to him.

Loach read:

'MOL 8814 BLUFF CHECK OMITTED TRUE CHECK OMITTED 92 NINETY-TWO MARCEL DISAPPEARED BELIEVED ARRESTED STOP LOUIS DISAPPEARED STOP KLEBER MISSING STOP SECOND RADIO SEIZED STOP IF PIERRE STILL WITH YOU DO NOT SEND HIM STOP ADIEU ADIEU ADIEU.

'It doesn't make sense,' said Loach.

'Sorry,' said Ince. 'It does.'

Loach read the message again.

'This may not even be genuine,' he said, weakly. 'There's no check.'

'She probably didn't have time,' said Ince.

'What about Simone?'

'She may still be active. All that's left of Jester. But she may be in a hell of a spot. You know Simone – not the sort of girl to say "adieu" three times.'

'Actually, I don't know her,' said Loach.

Ince seemed surprised.

'Don't you? I thought she was your operator the last time?'

'I had Auriol,' said Loach. 'Before he was switched to Talisman.'

Ince put the pink message back in the file.

'Of course, stupid of me,' he said. 'Simone was sent out after your return. Hell of a good girl.'

He returned the folder to the drawer.

Loach stood up, and went to the window. Ince was not used to people making free with his office, and getting up in the middle of interviews. But he said nothing.

'I still want to go,' said Loach.

'Of course.'

'I mean, today. Tonight.'

'I think that's impossible now.'

'It's all laid on, isn't it?' said Loach.

Ince decided it was time to be tougher.

'I don't think you quite understand,' he said. 'Your circuit has ceased to exist for the moment. I'm not even sure about your reception committee. They've made a point of asking you not to come – "do not send Pierre".'

'Nevertheless, I want to go.'

'The colonel's already made the decision,' said Ince. 'But I promise you that as soon as we've storted it out, you're top of the list.'

He produced his mirthless smile.

'I'm sure that you'll enjoy a few extra days in London. Flat's all right, is it?'

Loach turned from the window.

'Have you any idea how it's happened?'

Ince shook his head.

'Very sudden. They must have slipped up.'

'Or been betrayed?'

Ince was suddenly faceless.

'Quite possibly,' he said blandly.

'It's just the way it happened to Therese.'

'What do you know about Therese?' Ince asked very quietly.

'The same thing,' said Loach. 'Wiped out. Near Soissons.'

'And who told you?'

Loach exploded.

'Goddamn it, do you think we're all fools? That we don't meet and talk and hear things. Everybody knows about Therese.'

'Then you shouldn't talk about it,' said Ince primly.

Loach faced him.

'You really believe a whole circuit is destroyed, five people get the chop, and all it means is a pink slip in one of your bloody files? You really think that?'

'I think you need a drink,' said Ince. 'And I could do with it.'

From the sideboard under the curtained map, he produced a bottle of Scotch.

'No soda, I'm afraid,' apologized Ince. 'Clean out of it.'

Loach swallowed half his drink in one gulp.

'Couldn't get this stuff if it wasn't for our American comrades,' said Ince. 'God bless their PX.'

Loach said nothing.

'The best thing is for you to stay at the flat for the next forty-eight hours,' said Ince. 'By that time, we may know a lot more.'

Loach finished the other half.

'I would appreciate it – as a favour if, if you could send me as soon as possible,' he said.

'Of course,' said Ince.

'No I mean it. If Jester is smashed, we have to rebuild it. Maybe I could link up with Simone, if she's still around.'

'Could well be,' said Ince. 'Meanwhile, take the next couple of days and enjoy life. Don't brood. We'll soon have a new job for you.'

'Please.'

Loach seemed almost pathetic.

'And now paint the town a delicate shade of red,' smiled Ince, his eyes cold as ever.

'All I want is to get on with it,' said Loach. He wasn't smiling.

Ince stood up, and Loach went to the door.

'I'll ring you first thing in the morning,' he said.

'Do.'

Then a thought seemed to occur to Ince.

'Try to be at the flat round about six tonight, if it's not too much of a nuisance,' he said.

'Oh?'

'Nothing special – it's just that if we get any more news, I'll drop by and tell you. Won't keep you long in any event – if you have any plans for the evening.'

'I'll be in,' said Loach, and shut the door.

Ince went back to his desk. He seemed thoughtful. He picked up one of the two phones, and said:

'Get me the Park number.'

After a moment, somebody answered at the other end.

'Sylvia?' he said. 'Major Ince. I think we have a little job for you.'

3

Grau had just collected his new ration book, and now he was examining it as if it could tell him a thousand secrets.

For days he had worried about this morning. It meant filling in things, registration numbers, stamps, official codes.

In fact, it had been quite simple. A lot of fat women sitting behind trestle tables, looking self-important. He walked up to one of them, gave her his identity card and the filled-in form.

He watched her closely when he handed her his blue identity card. But she just took it, rubber-stamped the back, then filled in his name on the new ration book.

'There you are, Mr Harris,' said the stupid cow. 'Your clothing book and sweet coupons are inside.'

'Thank you,' he said meekly.

Now, in the little baker's shop he was enjoying a cup of coffee. He deserved it. Carefully he looked at the ration book.

Name: Harris. Initials: A. J. National Registration Number: ABQP 113 1.

Just as on his identity card.

Hartmann had been quite right, Grau admitted grudgingly. As long as the identity card fooled them, the rest was plain sailing.

'Try to get genuine documents when the opportunity comes,' Hartmann had told him. 'The identity card will open all doors.'

Grau had had his doubts. After all, everything about the card was false. The name did not exist. There was no Harris, A. J. for Arthur James. And ABQP 113 1 was a phoney number.

'Don't worry about it,' said Hartmann. 'As long as you're within the right age group, that letter code will see you through.'

'But when I collect my ration book and fill in false details, won't they spot them?' Grau had asked.

Hartmann, who loved his job in the false documentation branch of the Abwehr, had smiled condescendingly.

'My dear fellow,' he said. 'Forty-seven million people in that crowded little island, and you really think they'll check on each identity card number? Just stay out of trouble, and you'll be all right.'

And stayed out of trouble he certainly had, ever since U-310 had landed him ashore on a desolate part of the coast.

'You'll find it's much easier than you think,' Colonel Reinecke, chief of AMT VII, told him. 'We've laid it all on, and you should have no problems.'

'You can't take the British seriously,' Hartmann added. 'No pictures on their identity cards. Can you imagine that! And you don't report changes of address to the police – you tell the food officer!'

He collapsed with laughter.

Nevertheless, Grau had played it very safe all along. If he saw a drunk he crossed to the other side of the road. No point in getting involved in anything. A fight in a pub, or a witness in a street accident, or a row in a bus – it could mean the police, statements, showing your identity card, trouble.

So far, it had all gone splendidly.

Grau, on the whole, enjoyed his assignment. Not for him a drab, grey seaport or one of those ghastly smoke-covered industrial cities, endlessly watching ships, noting road convoys, extra trains, new military units. Grau was based in central London, and there could be worse places in which to be a spy.

He finished his coffee and decided to go to Selfridges, to register for his rations. He liked it there. For one thing, a big bustling food department meant that he avoided idle gossip with a little butcher down the road, or chat with a one-man grocery. Here it was impersonal, and he could collect his own 1*s* 1*d* worth of meat and his odd ounces of butter and cheese, and yet remain anonymous.

And Grau liked, above all things, to be anonymous.

There was another reason he liked the Oxford Street store. It gave him good reason to take a walk round Portman Square. And it never did any harm to keep an eye on Orchard Court, that big block of flats.

Grau knew what went on at Orchard Court. At least, he knew some of what went on. The whole Baker Street area was very interesting to him. Number 83, the red-bricked building, for example. And Bickenhall Mansions, and nearby Cumberland Mansions in Seymour Place.

Grau was a specialist. He made a point of becoming familiar with places like No 20 Grosvenor Square, or Chiltern Court, by the Underground station. Of course he never did it conspicuously – nobody took the slightest notice of him.

But he could tell so much from staff cars, and military gentlemen all too obviously dressed in civilian clothes, and motor-cycle messengers. The pubs were useful, so too were the tobacconist, newsagents, and the little cafés.

To Grau, the whole street scene was like a vast ocean containing many little fish. Fish who sometimes did not even know that they had been spotted, and hooked.

Grau bought his rations for a week, and outside took a No 8 bus to Shoot Up Hill. He let himself into the second-floor flat where he rented a room from a tedious widow who thought her Mr Harris was quite the ideal lodger.

'Is that you, Mr Harris?' she called out from the dining-room, where she was Hoovering the carpet.

'Yes, Mrs Croxley,' said Grau. 'And I got my new ration book.'

She came into the hall, a scarf round her head.

'Oh, you shouldn't have,' she said. 'I could have picked it up for you. All I would have needed was your identity card.'

If you but knew, Grau thought to himself.

But aloud he said:

'That's sweet of you, Mrs Croxley. But I had time, and I thought I might as well . . .'

'You should let me buy your rations in my little shop,' said Mrs Croxley. 'Actually, I think if I had your book, the butcher might let me have a little offal and things on the side . . . you know.'

Mrs Croxley gave a nervous giggle. It was the nearest she could ever get to being involved in a black market deal – two slices of liver, and maybe a kidney.

'Well, you see, being so near to the bookshop, it's quite easy for me to buy it all myself,' said Grau.

He wanted to change the subject. He hated having to explain minute little details which seemed so trivial to others, but which he had worked out so carefully.

Details which could mean his survival – or the hangman's rope in Wandsworth.

Grau was about to enter his room when Mrs Croxley called out:

'Oh, I've heard from Jimmy.'

'How is he?' asked Grau, as if he really cared.

'He might get a weekend off soon,' she said. 'I've got the spare room ready for him.'

'That'll be nice,' said Grau.

'He can't say much, of course, but they've been keeping him terribly busy. I worry myself sick.'

'But he's ground crew, Mrs Croxley,' said Grau. 'They don't fly.'

'I know, isn't it silly?' and she gave her nervous giggle.

No, the bastards don't fly, thought Grau savagely. They just load the bombs to drop on Frankfurt and Hamburg and Berlin.

'Would you like a cup of tea, Mr Harris?' asked Mrs Croxley.

'I'd love one,' said Grau.

He was just working out the date. There was a transmission due from Berlin tonight.

4

Loach walked up the narrow stairs and found himself in the small club-room. Marie, behind the bar, gave him a casual smile.

'Nice day,' she said.

Loach nodded, and ordered his drink. Only then did he notice Toussaint.

Toussaint was one of the Free French people, with de Gaulle's lot in Duke Street. They had little time for F Section, and the feeling had become mutual. There was a lot they knew about things in France, and one suspected they didn't pass it over.

But Loach was more interested in the girl with Toussaint. She was dark, had wet lips, and challenging breasts. Where had Toussaint found *her*?

'Join us,' said Toussaint, and because the girl was there, Loach did.

'Busy?' said Toussaint.

It could mean, are you just back from a mission? Or are you about to leave on one?

'So so,' said Loach. His eyes were on the girl.

'Oh, forgive me,' said Toussaint. 'Elise, Captain Loach. This is Elise.'

The wet lips smiled.

Loach waited for an explanation. But Toussaint had nothing more to say about Elise.

'I hear you have worries,' said Toussaint instead, casually, looking at Loach.

'*I* have worries?'

'I don't mean you. Your people.'

'Oh?'

'Problems.'

Out with it, thought Loach. Come out with it. What are you trying to say?

'Of course one must expect these things,' said Toussaint. 'You have trebled the circuits, haven't you.'

Loach's eyes narrowed. Toussaint noted his reaction.

'Oh, I see. Careless talk. Don't worry, my friend – we can talk freely in front of Elise. She knows everything.'

He corrected himself. 'She knows a lot.'

'Oh?'

'One of our cipher clerks.'

'But not one of ours,' said Loach, coldly.

Toussaint smiled at Elise.

'You would not think we are all Allies,' he said.

'I think your friend is quite right,' she said. 'We should not talk about these things. Not here.'

'If not here, where?' said Toussaint, looking round the little room.

Le Petit Club was the stamping-ground of the Duke Street lot. Sometimes F Section people, like Loach, drifted in. Because it was a membership club, strangers could, on the whole, be kept out. Here people whose names were pseudonyms and who were not supposed to know much about each other met and talked like salesmen discussing the day's markets.

But Loach, right now, was much more interested in the girl. When she spoke, her voice was husky. Her face was beautifully made up.

'Shall we go?' she said.

Toussaint raised his eyebrows.

'What's the hurry?'

'I want some lunch,' she said, and her invitation clearly did not include Loach.

Damn it, he thought, don't rush it. He'd like to get to know her more. Not only her, but perhaps her body. Given half a chance . . .

'Why don't we have a snack here?' suggested Loach.

She had taken command.

'He and I have things to talk over,' she said, and it was quite final.

Toussaint gave a sheepish grin.

'Sorry, you know how it is,' he said.

'Excuse me,' said the girl, and went to the powder-room.

'Nice girl,' said Loach, looking after her.

Nice was the last word he meant. Interesting he wanted to say. Sexy. Full of promise. Sensual. Hardly nice. But that's what he said.

'You want to know, is she special?' challenged Toussaint.

'I wouldn't mind seeing her again,' said Loach.

'Who knows?' said Toussaint. 'It's a small world.'

'She works in Duke Street?'

'She gets around,' said Toussaint, and you could take it any way you liked.

'When did she join you?'

'Quite early. In '40. She was one of the last to come over.'

Elise emerged from the small green-painted wooden door, and came to their table.

'We were just talking about you,' said Loach.

'I hope I was interesting,' she said. Then, to Toussaint: 'Ready?'

He nodded, and they left. She did not even look at Loach.

He crumpled up his cigarette packet. Blast it.

Marie, behind the bar, was washing some glasses. He speculated whether she'd be free tonight. No, of course not. She'd be working here.

He'd better find himself somebody. He needed it.

Loach got up, and left.

'*Au revoir*,' said Marie.

He never heard her.

Outside, it was clouding over slightly. Loach came out of St James's and turned into Piccadilly. He didn't quite know what he had in mind. Oh, yes, back at the flat at six. But till then...

He decided to have some lunch. It was a dull meal, five-shilling limit and all that, and the elderly waiter obviously disapproved of Loach, a healthy civilian in his thirites, living it up at the West End. You should be in Italy smashing the Hun, his nasty look hinted as he slammed down some watery soup. Or why aren't you in Burma, cleaning out the Japs, this with the boiled fish.

Loach left him a sixpenny tip with regret.

Then, in the bootmaker's shop near Burlington House, he saw what he realized he was looking for.

He spotted it in the window, and went straight into the shop.

'That riding crop, in the window, how much?' asked Loach.

The assistant fetched it, swished it for Loach's benefit.

'Very nice piece of craftsmanship,' he said.

'How much,' repeated Loach.

The man looked at the price tag.

'Two guineas.'

'I'll take it,' said Loach.

He paid, and the man gave him the wrapped riding crop.

'Not much chance for horse-riding these days, sir,' he said.

But Loach was already out of the shop.

5

Ince disdained the security coordination meetings. They sat round the table in the boardroom of the requisitioned hotel near Caxton Hall once a week, and if any of them really had something hot, he kept it to himself.

The naval commander from Combined Operations HQ always drummed his fingers after ten minutes, and Glover, from Economic Warfare, invariably doodled. The representative of STS, whose establishments trained the agents, liked the sound of his own voice, and the SPOC colonel, from special projects, just stared into space.

Ince wished the tea would hurry up. It was always brought in by two rather pretty ATS girls, who had been cleared back to their great-grandmother so that, after each meeting, they could tear the top sheet off his notepad, destroy all the doodles, and make sure that nobody had dropped any papers on the floor.

'We now have definite confirmation that AMT VII has its headquarters in the Hotel Lutetia on the Boulevard Raspail,' said Wilcox importantly. 'On the Left Bank, you know.'

Ince stared at him in disbelief. Either the man was an idiot, or he was taking them all for fools. AMT VII handled the repression of Allied agents in France – one of the Abwehr's key sections. And Orchard Court had known about the Hotel Lutetia for two years, at the least.

Ince thought he might make some caustic remark, and shoot down Wilcox in flames. But he dismissed the idea. What was the point anyway? To impress Glover, or the SPOC colonel?

The general who chaired these meetings looked at his watch.

I bet he's also wondering what's happened to the tea, thought Ince.

Like Glover, he found he had been doodling – a winged cupid, no less, firing arrows into space.

Ince allowed himself a thin smile.

Loach kept coming back into his mind.

A good man, Loach. He had now completed two missions across the Channel. And the way he had planned and executed the blowing up of that train near Chartres was a model to all.

Executed – that was quite Freudian. It had been a troop train, after all, and reports had spoken of 153 German soldiers killed, and many wounded.

Loach had seemed a bit on edge. Had he had enough? Was

he seeing spooks under the bed? Maybe 'Pierre' should be rested.

'Gentlemen, tea,' said the general.

And there they were, the two tall, slim ATS girls, putting a cup down by each of them, with one biscuit in each saucer.

When they had left, and there had been a stirring of cups, and sipping of tea the general cleared his throat.

'We've had a good meeting,' he said, 'and I will report the points made to our lords and masters.'

Points made? You must be joking, thought Ince. Like the Hotel Lutetia being Abwehr headquarters?

The general pushed his cup to one side.

'We're all aware, I think, that things are moving,' he said. 'We've sent some two thousand people in so far, but that mustn't make us over-confident. Security is more vital than ever.'

Here comes the weekly sermon, thought Ince.

'Home security reports a significant increase in illict Morse signals within the UK.'

Ah, for once something interesting.

'I'm sure we can leave it to our people. But there are bound to be one or two agents they haven't pin-pointed yet.'

The general looked round grimly, as if one of them might be sitting round the table.

Ince took the plunge.

'These illegal radio transmissions – any special patterns emerging?'

'That's a matter for home security, Major Ince,' said the general curtly. 'Just tell your own organizations to be on the alert. And if any of you smell a rat, get after it.'

What a charming way of putting it, thought Ince.

6

In the small, shabby pub behind the bustle of Oxford Circus, Grau sipped his uninspiring English beer. He'd never get to like this stuff, but it was so beautifully anonymous. You asked for half a pint, and you were one of them. It was almost like a pass. 'Half a bitter, please,' and nobody gave you a second look.

This was the time of day when Schindler crept in. The only reason Grau cultivated this pub was because of the nervous little man in the ill-fitting raincoat.

Schindler was a tailor, and he worked in a clothing manufacturer's place in Margaret Street. That made it sound too grand, really. It was the tailor's workshop, employing about a dozen people. 'Wholesale Only' it said on the door.

Grau was very interested in this workshop. He had discovered that all the people who worked there were, like Schindler, refugees. Continentals.

And the thing that intrigued him was that they made continental clothes. Suits in foreign materials, cut in the French, Dutch, German way. Everything painstakingly foreign, the lapels, the buttons, the stitching.

It had taken Grau a long time to find out, but when he did all the effort was worth it.

And when Grau discovered that one of the little people came to this pub, the rest was not too difficult.

Actually, this was one of the occasions when Grau took a degree of risk. To create a relationship with Schindler, Grau adopted the pose of himself being a German refugee. He did it subtly – but it gave Schindler a fellow feeling.

Normally, Grau's English was impeccable, but he allowed himself a trace of a German accent when talking to the little tailor. Sometimes he'd slip in the odd German word, and then they'd both look round the pub, like two naughty schoolboys caught in the act. Nobody took the slightest notice, but it didn't seem right, using German in the heart of London in the middle of the war, surrounded by all these people.

And it created a bond between them.

Grau had a good idea who wore the clothes Schindler and his friends made so painstakingly. British agents, sent into Europe by the gentlemen in Orchard Court.

No good giving a man the finest forged identity papers if he wore a suit made by the Fifty Shilling Tailors, cut in finest Kilburn High Street style. So Orchard Court got continental materials in the continental style – by continental tailors. Ten minutes from Oxford Circus.

Grau would love to see the order book. It would give him childish joy. Obviously, they wouldn't have the names of the agents in it, but it would be interesting to see if, for example, there was a rush order for half a dozen French working-class suits, or a jacket and trousers, Dutch style, were urgently needed.

And there he was.

Schindler came in, and when he saw Grau, he gave him a little wave, and came over.

'A beer?' said Grau.

Schindler nodded and sat down wearily. Grau got the half pint from the counter, and set it in front of Schindler.

'Prosit,' said Grau, greatly daring.

'Cheers,' said Schindler.

He took a sip.

'Gets worse every day,' said Grau.

'Can't expect a Dortmunder,' said Schindler, and gave a wan smile.

Grau was intrigued by this man. Schindler had fled to Britain in 1938 from Stuttgart, having lost his tailor's business to the Nazis. He was a good craftsman, and found himself a job with a bespoke tailor in Willesden.

War broke out, and Schindler was promptly arrested, and interned by the British in the Isle of Man. He had a rough time – there were some real Nazis in the camp, and two of them shared Schindler's hut. They liked beating up the little Jew, and there were times when Schindler wondered why he had ever bothered to flee from the Reich.

Then somebody at the Home Office took another look at his file, and after a year behind barbed wire, Schindler was released.

And found himself making fake clothes for British Intelligence.

Grau didn't hate Jews, but aspects of Schindler aggravated him. The way the man, with his atrocious German accent, had adopted English phrases like 'old boy' and 'oh dear' and 'cheers'. The way this fellow, who obviously preferred cream cakes and chocolate and roll mops, made his daily pilgrimage to this ghastly pub, and drank his English beer just like one of these bloody Cockneys.

Why the hell was he so keen to be as British as British? What had they done to him, apart from putting him inside a prison camp?

'Busy?' asked Grau.

'Orders, orders, nothing but orders,' said Schindler.

'You must make me a suit some time,' said Grau. He had never let on, of course, that he knew what kind of tailoring went on in that workshop. As far as Schindler was concerned, Grau thought he was just another tailor working on customers' orders.

'You'll have a long wait, my friend,' said the tailor.

'Not to worry, it'll take me that long to save enough coupons.'

'One day,' said Schindler, 'I will make the most beautiful English suits – better than Savile Row.'

But he didn't elaborate.

A GI came into the pub with a girl on each arm. He took one look at the gloomy, musty place.

'Jesus,' said the GI.

'Come on, Johnny, take us to Rainbow Corner,' said one of the girls, nuzzling up to him.

'Jesus,' said the GI, and they all rushed out.

'Our Allies,' said Schindler sadly.

Grau thought that was rich. 'Our' Allies, coming from him.

But aloud he said:

'Some are brave boys. The pilots.'

'Of course,' said Schindler. He took another sip and Grau knew what was coming.

'Cheers,' said Schindler.

Grau nearly bit his lip.

'How's the book business?' asked Schindler suddenly.

It took Grau by surprise.

'Oh, not bad,' he said. 'Not much else people can do in the blackout.'

'I'm usually too tired to read,' said Schindler. 'After a day in the workshop.'

'And I suppose you can't get people – skilled people?'

'We only use continentals—'

And then Schindler stopped. That was something they had told him never to mention.

'Oh?' said Grau, totally disinterested.

'What I mean is, we use anybody we can get. Not like the old days.'

'Have the other half,' suggested Grau.

'Actually, it is my round, old boy,' said Schindler. Then he saw the clock.

'Actually, would you mind – if I left it till the next time?'

'Of course not. You have somewhere to go?'

Schindler was very apologetic.

'It is Beethoven's *Eroica* on the radio tonight. I want to get home in time.'

Grau nodded, full of understanding.

'Go on. You owe me one.'

Schindler gave him a grateful look, and shuffled out.

Grau pondered. It hadn't yielded much, but it was one more useful tightening of the links.

Anyway, didn't the British have that excellent saying: softly, softly, catchee monkey.

7

Loach drew the blackout curtains, and flung himself into one of the armchairs. It was well after six, but no sign of Ince.

What had he said? '...if we get any more news, I'll drop by...'

Loach was anxious to hear that news, if there was any. Had Simone survived? Adieu, adieu, adieu was hardly the customary way of signing off. It suggested she knew AMT VII was close at hand.

He wondered about Simone. Curious the way Ince had thought they had worked together – but then with as many as thirty-five circuits on his mind at any time, Ince could be forgiven such an error.

He looked at his watch: 6.20.

Still no Ince.

This girl Simone. Maybe he *did* know her. Perhaps they had met on a training course. Or on a test exercise. That was one of the peculiar things about the organization – a lot of people knew each other, and yet they didn't. Faces were familiar, but names unknown. You attended a radio class with somebody, sat next to them at a briefing, didn't see them again for months. Then, maybe, in a pub – or a café in a French market town. Sometimes you stared at each other blankly, occasionally you risked a flicker of recognition.

Simone, of course, wouldn't be her name. Any more than Pierre was his.

Restless, Loach picked up the thin, page-rationed evening paper. US Air Force planes had dropped a total of 24,000 tons of bombs on German aircraft factories in the last four weeks, blazed a communiqué. And Berlin had had its heaviest night raid. A mutual aid agreement signed with the Free French.

That was rich, thought Loach. Mutual aid – when Orchard House and Duke Street weren't even talking to each other.

A man called Peron had been appointed war minister in Argentine. A Nottingham man had been fined £1 for giving bread to pigeons. A woman wrote to the editor, protesting angrily that slacks needed eight coupons, but skirts only seven. 'I have to climb stairs, and I must wear slacks in the factory,' she moaned.

And Luton was suffering from a beer shortage.

Where the hell is Ince? thought Loach.

If things had gone according to plan, Loach would now be getting kitted out, ready for the flight into France. He'd be putting on the specially made and worn-looking French suit, with the frayed shirt and faded tie to match. They'd put him through the final check to make sure he didn't have anything incriminating on him, like a packet of Players, or an English matchbox. They'd give him a different watch, and his identity papers, and ration documents, all beautifully authentic, on the surface.

He didn't quite know how he felt about the mission being cancelled. Let down, of course. He had nerved himself up to the thing, and now felt a little lost. Or was he lying to himself? Wasn't he really bloody relieved? Well, wasn't he?

Steady now.

I wonder if they have any brandy in this place?

Loach went over to the likely looking cabinet, and opened the doors. Good God, they had. He examined the bottle. The real thing. Cognac!

'You bastards think of everything, don't you,' he muttered, and smiled grimly. Well, he didn't know who paid for it all, the secret defence estimates, or the Intelligence budget, but that bottle was going to be a lot more empty . . .

The door buzzer sounded.

Good, Ince.

Loach opened the door. The girl smiled at him.

'Colette?' she said.

'I'm sorry . . .'

Loach was baffled.

'I'm Sylvia,' said the girl. Her perfume was delicious.

'Oh yes,' said Loach, stupidly.

'Well, can't I come in?' she said charmingly – and entered.

'I don't know – anybody called Colette,' said Loach, and then realized that he still had the bottle of cognac in his hand. He put it down as if it was red-hot.

'She lives here,' said the girl.

'Not now,' said Loach. 'I mean, not at the moment.'

Was it some girl from the section who had stayed here? Colette sounded just right. But who was this?

'She must be on a job,' said the girl. 'You must think me an idiot.'

'Not at all,' said Loach.

She is quite something, he thought. Simply dressed, but to the utmost effect. Great legs. Slim ankles. Was it true what they said about girls with slim ankles – that they are better in bed?

'Are you her boyfriend?' asked the girl.

'I don't know Colette,' repeated Loach.

She smiled understandingly.

'Of course, forgive me.'

He looked puzzled.

'One must never know anybody, must one?' she said. 'It's one of the rules. Sorry.'

She put her head to one side and looked at him quizzically.

'Yes,' she said. 'You're her type.'

Loach had to laugh.

'That's very nice, but you're making a mistake. I've never had the pleasure.'

She seemed disappointed.

'You know, I'm beginning to believe you. I've goofed again. I'm terribly sorry.'

She turned to the door. That perfume was quite something.

'Look . . .' said Loach.

But she was obviously anxious to save him further embarrassment.

'I'll call some other time – when Colette is back,' she smiled.

She reached out and opened the door herself.

Ince stood there.

He looked from her to Loach.

'I had no idea you knew Sylvia,' he said, and came in.

'I came round to see Colette,' said the girl. 'I burst in on this poor man, Major. Will you tell him I'm not Mata Hari.'

Ince allowed himself a smile.

'Sylvia is – quite all right,' he said. 'A very nice girl, Loach.'

'Of course,' said Loach. What the devil was going on?

'You need have no worries about Sylvia,' said Ince. 'She's in the picture.'

'I see,' said Loach. 'That's good.'

He didn't know what to say.

'I thought Colette was staying here,' said the girl.

'Captain Loach is temporarily in residence,' said Ince.

'Oh, of course.'

She nodded, as if that explained everything.

Ince, all benign, turned to Loach.

'I'm off. I just wanted to tell you I don't think we'll know any more till the morning.'

'Nothing else has come in?' asked Loach.

'Nothing definite,' said Ince, vaguely. 'But we've had very little time.'

'Would you like a brandy?' asked Loach.

'Another time,' said Ince. He gave them both a look. 'Enjoy yourselves. Goodnight, Sylvia. See you tomorrow, Loach.'

He closed the front door behind him.

'Well,' said the girl. 'Mutual friends. Surprise, surprise. But then I don't suppose anybody else would be staying in this place.'

'Do – do please stay if you want to,' said Loach. 'I mean, if you're not in a rush . . .'

'Thank you,' she said.

She sat down in the other armchair, kicked off her shoes, and tucked her legs beneath her.

'You work for – the Section?' said Loach.

She settled back in the armchair cosily.

'I'd like that brandy you offered him,' she said.

8

They had dinner in a small restaurant in Soho which somehow managed to keep the war at bay, once one passed through the blackout curtain. Each table had tiny lamps with red shades, and it was a place where a lot of couples went on the last night of his leave – or the first meeting.

Loach found this girl tremendously attractive. She had enough reserve to make her a shade mysterious, and yet she seemed interested in whatever he said.

She never asked about his job, or the Section. She was well trained.

Loach wondered about her. Was she F Section? Ciphers maybe? Not field operations, surely. And yet?

'My father's a vicar,' she said, with an impish glint.

'A vicar!'

'Why? Does it seem that unlikely?'

'No, not at all. Just that—'

'It's just that it's the last thing you'd expect my father to be.'

'Well, I . . .'

Loach gave up.

'You're quite right,' she said. 'He doesn't approve either. I haven't heard from him for four years.'

'Doesn't approve of the work you do?'

She didn't rise to it.

'Doesn't approve, that's all.'

Loach lit her cigarette.

'You're a bit nervous,' she said, half jokingly, half serious.

'Nervous?'

'Your hand – it shook a bit.'

'I'm perfectly fit,' he snapped. 'I only had a medical five days ago.'

Suddenly she was too understanding.

'I didn't mean anything like that,' she said gently.

'Oh, I'm sorry,' he said. 'Sometimes, things . . .'

'Of course,' she said.

She put her hand over his on the table.

Loach, quite cold-bloodedly, was studying her.

Her neck, the promise of her breasts. He noticed her wedding ring.

'Married?'

'No.'

She was very curt.

'Engaged?'

'No.'

The ring puzzled him.

'It's none of my business,' he apologized.

'You mean this,' and she held up her hand with the wedding ring.

'I'm sorry,' said Loach.

'I'm not even a widow,' she said. 'You don't have to be sorry.'

'Why the ring?'

'It helps a girl these days,' she said, matter-of-fact. 'In awkward situations. It has its uses.'

You're quite a hard bitch, thought Loach. He didn't like himself for it.

'I'm not either,' he said.

'You're not what?'

'Married.'

'I don't really care,' she said.

'Have you known Colette long?' he asked after a pause.

'Long enough.'

After that, he made small talk about this and that and found her to be good fun. They had quite a chat about *Gone With the Wind*, and what Clark Gable did for women and Vivien Leigh for men. She thought Betty Grable was common. He said she had a nice body.

Later, he made one more attempt.

'Do you know many people in – in Major Ince's lot?'

She was quite cool again.

'If I did, should I tell you?'

'He gave you very high references.'

'You mean, he said I am "quite all right". Wasn't that it? "You need have no worries about me". So you can relax.'

'You sound a little bitter.'

'You're quite wrong,' she smiled.

'Ince is a funny bloke,' said Loach.

'Is he?'

'I don't know what he uses in place of emotion.'

'I'm quite sure he makes out,' she said.

Loach paid the bill, and outside in the dark they searched for a taxi. One was stolen under their noses in Shaftesbury Avenue, but in Cambridge Circus they did the same thing to a Polish airman and his blonde.

Loach felt a little drunk. They had had several brandies earlier in the evening, and he had drunk most of the wine during the dinner.

'Come back to the flat,' he said.

'Why not,' she said.

9

In Maddox Street, Grau had picked himself up a girl. The anonymity of his task did not allow him to establish a permanent relationship with a woman. Grau was word perfect when it came to his cover role, but it was safer never to lie unless he had to. A girlfriend would want to know his address, where he worked, why he wasn't in the forces, where he was born, whether his parents were around, where he went to school, did he have any brothers or sisters.

He'd spend his evening spinning a fine tissue of trivial lies, and that sooner or later would mean slipping up. Not that she would rush off to Scotland Yard, but it might cause complications. Far better to avoid them.

So when Grau needed sex, he bought it, like his cheese ration.

And the blacked-out West End was a good place to make his purchases.

She was standing in a doorway in Maddox Street, quite openly jingling a bunch of keys, and as he came level to her, she said:

'Are you looking for a naughty girl, *chéri*?'

It always amused Grau the way they dressed up their approach. But these girls obviously knew their customers. 'Would you like a tart? How about a quick fuck?' Would hardly do fifty yards from Regent Street.

Once, near Hay's Mews, a sweet little girl had asked him out of the shadows: 'Are you lonely?'

That had struck such a chord he still remembered it. And he had given her two extra pounds afterwards, just for putting it like that.

This one now belonged to the universal order of whores. Grau knew that he could pick her up in Montparnasse, or on the Moselle Strasse in Frankfurt, in Rome or in Brussels. She had a French accent, had been imported into London, and would cost him £5 for an hour, and not a minute more.

'Where?' asked Grau.

'In my flat, round the corner,' she smiled.

'All right,' said Grau.

She immediately linked her arm in his, and guided him.

'I like you,' she said. 'You will warm me up?'

There's no need to make out I excite you, thought Grau wearily. You really don't have to put on an act.

She led him to a front door, unlocked it, and went up some stairs.

'Come along, *chéri*,' she said. 'Only one flight.'

On the landing, she called out 'Yoohoo,' like a housewife back from shopping. A crone with red hair appeared. The tart disappeared in a room on the left, and the crone gave Grau a business-like smile.

'Five pounds,' she said. Market price.

Grau gave her five pounds, and five shillings for herself.

'Very kind,' she said. 'She'll be ready for you.'

And she was. When Grau entered the door on the left, he found himself in a bare room – bare except for one bed, a chair, and a side-board with a dirty mirror.

Stuck in the frame of the mirror was a photograph. An American soldier, in jump boots.

'My boyfriend,' said the tart proudly. 'He is a parachutist.'

She had stripped to her black lace underwear, and was sitting expectantly on the edge of the bed. Grau noticed there were no pillows.

'Take your clothes off, *chéri*,' she suggested.

Grau was already doing so, but he wished it was a simpler process, undressing before a tart's eyes. He'd like to pull a zip, and shed everything, get on with it, then step into his clothes, zip them up, and out.

'You are English?' she asked.

'Yes,' said Grau. He knew it was only small talk for her customers.

'Merchant Navy?'

That surprised him. Why did she think that?

'I love sailors,' she said, hardly giving him a chance to reply.

That's tough on your paratrooper friend, thought Grau, taking off his pants.

She had unclipped her bra, and was now beginning to remove the rest.

'Come,' she said. 'Make me very tired.'

Grau did.

He left quite some time before the hour was up. As he went down the sairs, the crone maid called after him, 'Goodbye – see you again.'

Obviously she had appreciated her tip.

But she'd wait in vain for the next time.

Grau made a point of never picking up the same girl twice.

That way they'd never get to know him.

10

When Loach produced the riding crop, Sylvia thought: 'Oh my God, he's one of those.'

They were both naked, and she was lying on the bed. Loach had got up to get some brandy, but when he returned to the bedroom he held the crop.

Sylvia was a professional, which meant that nothing shocked her in her trade.

If they wanted to be loved, she loved them. If they wanted to be beaten, she beat them.

After they returned to the flat, they had both drunk some more.

Loach had kissed her, and then they had gone into the bedroom.

Loach made love to her like a man released from prison. He was neither gentle nor kind, and he hurt Sylvia.

Afterwards, they each smoked a cigarette.

'Did you enjoy that?' she asked.

He turned his head, and stared at her, coldly.

'Did you?' he asked.

She stretched, and gave a purr. It was a good way of suggesting he was a great lover, without having to say anything she didn't feel.

But he reacted strangely.

'You wanted this, didn't you?' he said.

'This?'

'To go to bed with me?'

She couldn't help but laugh at the conceit of the man.

'What's so funny?' he snapped.

'You,' she said. 'I'm not that hard up, you know.'

He leant on one elbow. His face was unpleasant. She decided she had to head him off, quickly.

'I went to bed with you because I wanted to,' she said. 'Don't you see? That's why I am here, you chump. I like you.'

He lay back again, staring at the ceiling.

'You have a good body,' he said.

She remembered what he said in the restaurant.

'As good as Betty Grable?'

'Shut up,' he said.

He's on edge, she decided. He's got problems.

Loach, instead of being relaxed, felt growing excitement. He was looking forward to what was coming. He had planned to do it with a woman that night, and here she was.

'Would you like a drink?' he asked her.

'I don't mind. What time is it?'

He still had his watch on.

'Just before two.'

'No sirens tonight,' she said languidly. The Luftwaffe was paying a few odd visits.

'I'll get us something,' he said, and got up.

'Do you have to be early in the morning?' she asked.

'I keep office hours.'

'Lucky man.'

'Glad you think so,' he said.

He went through the door, and when he came back he'd got the riding crop.

'Get up,' he said.

'What's the matter with you?' said Sylvia. She suddenly felt scared.

'Get up,' he repeated. He stood there, flexing the riding crop.

'Come to bed,' she said.

Quite suddenly, he lashed out. The whip caught across an arm. She gave a cry.

'That hurt!'

'Get up,' he said, for the third time.

She sat up in the bed, staring at him.

'I think you need that drink,' she said, holding her arm.

'You bitch,' he said, but without hate, almost endearingly.

And he struck her across the face with the crop.

She screamed, more with the shock than the pain. She touched her face – she could feel a cut.

Loach stood over her, enjoying himself. There was a drop of perspiration on his forehead. He was breathing a little heavily. He was quite naked, and he held the riding crop poised.

'You're mad,' she said, and jumped up, panic-stricken.

'Ah,' he said, as if she was doing just the right thing.

He laid into her with the riding crop, slashing and hitting and she screamed and tried to cover herself, but without success.

One blow caught her across the right breast, leaving a thin red line, with some blood seeping through, and she shrieked as she had never done in her life.

For one wild moment she tried to grab at the whip, snatch it from him, but he just pushed her against the wall and laughed.

A chair overturned.

Again he hit her, and now she knew her life was at stake.

She ran for the door.

'Don't you enjoy it?' he shouted.

She was like an animal at bay, shaking, terrified, her hair straggling down, perspiration on her body, and those vicious marks where the whip had caught her, in her face, on her breast, on the arms.

'Please don't,' she pleaded.

'Bitch,' said Loach. And he struck her with all his strength.

She saw the brandy bottle, and threw it at him. He laughed.

She ran to the window and tried to rip open the blackout curtains. But he was right behind her, and laid into her back.

Again and again, the whip came down lashing thin welts into her flesh.

Once more she screamed.

It was the scream of a woman who knew she was alone with death.

And death was naked.

Loach was past caring. This was what he needed. This was what he had craved.

He raised the riding crop. It was well-bloodstained.

11

Ince walked into the police station, and asked for the detective inspector whose name he had been given.

They showed him into the office, and the inspector waved him into a chair.

'Nasty business, sir,' he said. 'Tea?'

'Thank you,' said Ince, and the inspector poured him some from a Thermos.

'One of your men?'

'Captain Loach is one of our officers,' said Ince, deliberately vaguely.

'He said he was a captain.'

Ince asked: 'Where is he now?'

'In the cells.'

'And the woman?'

'St Mary Abbott's Hospital. Not too good.'

'How did the police get involved?' asked Ince, as if, really, it wasn't any of their business.

The inspector looked at a typed sheet in front of him.

'Emergency call from neighbours in the mews. 2.43 AM. They heard a woman screaming. Sound of breaking glass. Dialled 999. We found the lady lying in the hall, collapsed. Badly hurt. Your Captain Loach said there had been' – and the inspector read from the sheet – ' "a lovers' tiff". The officers weren't satisfied and arrested him. An ambulance took her to hospital. She was unconscious. When we brought him here he said, 'You'd better call my people.' He gave us your Welbeck number.'

'I see,' said Ince, cursing.

'The lady was naked,' said the inspector, 'and your bloke wasn't wearing much either. We found this in the bedroom.'

The inspector put a Cellophane-wrapped riding crop on the desk in front of Ince.

'I think you can take it for granted this caused her injuries.'

Ince was thinking hard.

‘What happens now?’ he asked.

Christ, thought the inspector. Bloody callous outfit, this lot.

‘We’re waiting to take a statement from the woman, when she comes to,’ he said. ‘Meanwhile, we’ll charge your man, and ask for a remand. If he gets bail, we’ll ask you to provide an escort and keep him confined until the next hearing.’

‘I don’t think he’d better be charged,’ said Ince quietly.

‘I beg your pardon, Major?’

‘It would be better if this doesn’t come up in court.’

‘I don’t feel you quite understand, sir,’ said the inspector patiently. ‘Your man has committed a very serious assault. Grievous bodily harm.’

‘I understand perfectly,’ said Ince.

‘I know how you must feel about Captain Loach,’ said the inspector kindly. ‘But I wouldn’t worry. They’ll look after him.’

‘No, we’ll do that.’

It was a statement, not a request.

The inspector got up.

‘I’m sorry, sir, that’s out of my hands. I am going to charge this man with GBH and he will appear at West London Magistrate’s Court later this morning. I suggest you be there, sir. Southcombe Street. Opposite Cadby Hall.’

‘I think you ought to know this matter involves national security,’ said Ince softly.

It had the desired effect.

‘Ah,’ said the inspector. You couldn’t be a divisional CID officer in Kensington in wartime and not have a healthy respect for those two words – and the power they implied.

‘We will see to it that the interests of justice are fully met,’ said Ince. ‘But none of this must reach a court.’

‘Hmm,’ said the inspector. ‘I don’t know what the superintendent will say.’

‘My masters will talk to your masters,’ said Ince.

‘And what about the young lady? She may want to bring charges.’

'She will not,' said Ince.

'You know her, sir?'

'She will not prefer any charges,' said Ince firmly.

The inspector didn't like any of it.

'And what happens to Captain Loach now?' he asked.

'You will release him to us.'

The inspector made a last-ditch stand.

'I'll have to consult my superiors,' he said.

'Please do.'

The inspector gave up.

'Will you make the arrangements for an escort, then?'

Ince smiled his thin smile.

'I'll sign for him,' he said. He made ready to leave.

'You realize this man needs – he may well need treatment,' said the inspector.

'I'm sure everything will be taken care of, Inspector,' said Ince smoothly.

The inspector went to his desk and looked at the folder on it.

'You're in Marylebone, aren't you, sir? Near Baker Street?'

'Yes, quite handy,' said Ince.

'And what exactly is your unit, sir? ISRB No 1?'

'Rather boring,' said Ince. 'Inter Services Research Bureau. Thanks for the tea.'

12

The last thing Loach expected was to be driven to Ince's office in a staff car. No escort. No handcuffs.

He was asked to wait in an ante-chamber with a 1943 copy of *Picture Post* lying on the radiator. Rather like waiting for the dentist.

He was still hazy about what had happened. Now that it was over, he felt quite normal. If only the bitch hadn't made so much noise. Then the police...

It would mean a court-martial, of course. At least, that's what he thought until he was called into Ince's office. There was a bald man sitting in the other visitor's chair. It was all very informal.

'Sit down, Loach,' said Ince affably.

Loach looked from one to the other.

'Oh, this is Mr Cleaver,' said Ince. 'Works on the second floor.'

Loach nodded. But the second floor meant nothing to him.

'Got yourself in a bit of a mess last night, didn't you?' said Ince, offering him a cigarette.

Loach was staggered how casually he took it.

'I – I don't know what to say, sir,' he replied.

'Perhaps it's best you shouldn't say too much,' said Ince gently. 'To anyone ...'

'I really don't know what happened,' said Loach. 'I mean – we both had too much to drink, of course.'

Ince nodded.

'I don't know what they're going to charge me with,' said Loach.

'You're not on any charge,' said Ince.

'After – after what happened?'

'Nobody wants any charges,' said Ince. He smiled coldly at Loach. 'Nobody.'

For a moment, Loach didn't know what to say. Then:

'How's Sylvia?' asked Loach. It was the first time he had inquired about her.

'Still in hospital. But she'll be all right,' said Ince.

'I must send her some flowers.'

'That would be nice, Captain Loach.'

It was the first time Cleaver had spoken.

Loach shifted uneasily.

'Isn't there really going to be any kind of trouble? The police?'

'Let me worry about that,' said Ince.

'It wasn't very pleasant, sitting in that cell.'

'Still, compares favourably with Fresnes? Or the Hotel Lutetia?' smiled Cleaver, encouragingly.

Loach wished he knew what the man did.

'Oh yes. It's not the Gestapo.'

He puffed his cigarette.

'Was she – was she very bad?'

Ince was quite cool about it.

'You gave her a nasty going over,' he said.

'Not very nice, is it?' said Loach, looking from one to the other.

'We're men of the world, all three of us,' said Cleaver cordially. 'We all have our own little – quirks. I wouldn't lose any sleep about it.'

The man puzzled Loach.

'It was just something that – that came over me . . .'

'You had had a lot to drink,' said Cleaver.

'Exactly.'

'And you've been through a lot, in the last eighteen months, haven't you? The last time across wasn't a rest cure.'

'I think the mission being called off so suddenly – that was the biggest strain. The whole business about Jester – the circuit being wiped out,' said Loach. He remembered something.

'Any news about Simone? Is she safe?'

Ince nodded.

'She's all right,' he said.

Loach seemed to relax.

'Well, if there aren't going to be any repercussions about this business, I'd like to get going as soon as possible.'

'That's a very good idea,' said Cleaver.

'We may have some orders for you this afternoon,' said Ince.

Loach stood up.

'Thank you, sir,' he said.

There was something else he wanted to say. He took the plunge.

'I must say, everybody is being very decent about last night –

especially the organization. I thought I was going inside for years.'

'Just because of an unfortunate disagreement with a girlfriend?' said Cleaver, as if it didn't matter a damn.

'Bit more than that, I'm afraid,' said Loach. He added hastily: 'She's not my girlfriend, of course.'

He walked over to Ince's desk and crushed his cigarette in the ashtray.

'As far as we're concerned, the incident is closed,' said Ince. 'Come back at three.'

Loach nodded at them both, and left.

Ince looked at the bald man.

'Well?'

'I hate snap decisions,' said Cleaver.

'We need one.'

'He's a ruthless bastard.'

'Good. That's his job.'

'He is not crazy, or anything.'

'Good.'

'But I think he's twisted.'

Ince showed his teeth.

'You've seen a lot of us. Do you think Loach is the only one who's twisted, as you put it?'

Cleaver scratched his nose.

'You've got a job for this man? I mean, across the Channel?'

Ince nodded.

'I know I mustn't ask details, but does it involve women? Will he be working with women?'

'Yes.'

'In close contact?'

'The closest. He may spend days with one in an attic, or hide out with her in a hayloft or a hotel room at the back of the Gare du Nord – that kind of thing.'

'Do you know the woman?'

'Yes.'

'Is she attractive?'

'Very.'
Cleaver was interested.
'How do your people manage in that kind of situation? Posing as man and wife in one bedroom, or being stuck in a confined space?'
'Sex, you mean?'
'Of course,' said Cleaver.
'You're supposed to tell us that. After all, you're our tame psychiatrist.'
'You have lots of case-histories, you must have.'
Ince shrugged his shoulders.
'It goes on the whole time. It can get pretty boring, when you're holed up. But there's one thing that's more important to them.'
'Freud would be interested to hear that. What is it?'
'They want to stay alive,' said Ince.
'Ah,' said Cleaver. Then, after a pause:
'In that case, I'd keep Loach well away from it. The man is a sadist – a girl in his power, anything could happen.'
'I'm supposed to tell the colonel that? It sounds like Victorian melodrama.'
'You asked me,' said Cleaver. 'And you should ask that girl in hospital. I understand she'll have some scars for life.'
'Doesn't leave us much choice, does it?'
'None at all, in my view,' said Cleaver. 'You're not surprised, are you?'
'Nothing surprises me in this place,' said Ince.

13

The colonel put the folder down.
'That's it, then,' he said.
Ince waited for what was coming.
'Pity. He's a good man.'
'Yes, sir.'

'Who fixed him up with Sylvia?'

'I did, sir.'

'Why?'

'The usual reason, sir. He needed relaxing. He was on edge. And he's a loner. He doesn't seem to have a girlfriend on tap. In any case, we don't want them to bring their crumpet to the safe houses.'

The colonel stroked the folder in front of him.

'That's why we have the girls set up, isn't it, sir?'

'All right, Ince. Point made. She's completely reliable?'

'Absolutely.'

'And we're looking after her?'

'Yes, sir. The 311 file.'

The colonel sighed.

'If it had to happen, I suppose it was better here than in the field.'

'That's the whole point, sir. If he did it to his radio operator in a French *pension*, you could imagine the rest . . .'

The blue phone buzzed. It was not as urgent as the other two, green and red, and the colonel simply said:

'Not at the moment.'

He put the receiver back.

'About Loach.'

'Sir?'

'Is he sick? Does he need treatment?'

'Cleaver says he's quite sane. You've seen his report. Just twisted sexually.'

'Sane!'

'Cleaver is speaking as a psychiatrist, sir.'

'I often wonder which side they're on.'

Ince decided it was better to remain silent.

'Didn't we have any suspicions? Was there nothing that could have given us a clue?'

'No,' said Ince. 'I've been through his whole record.'

'Well then – why suddenly now?'

'Fatigue, sir. Loach has been through a lot. He can probably still control it when everything's going well. But put him under strain ...'

The colonel had made his decision.

'All right. What do you propose?'

'Inverloch, sir.'

The colonel nodded.

'You want authority?'

'Please, sir.'

'What will you tell Loach?'

'The usual. Or something like it.'

'It seems to work.'

'So far.'

'All right then, Major.'

'Thank you, sir. May I?'

And he reached over and took the file from the colonel.

'When will Loach know?' asked the colonel.

'This afternoon, sir. He expects to be given new orders.'

'He should find them interesting,' said the colonel.

14

Grau was very depressed. The latest instructions from Germany made him wonder if it was all worth while. They informed him that there was an establishment, in a small street off St James's, called Le Petit Club. It was frequented by the Free French from Duke Street and many of the SOE people. The department was interested in this place, so the instructions informed Grau.

So what the devil did they want him to do? Put on a false moustache, a phoney French accent and become a member?

Or poison the barman and take his job, so that he could overhear the chatter?

What depressed Grau was that he knew all about Le Petit Club. It was hardly very secret. He would also be very foolish to go near it. And if he did, what would he find out?

Sometimes Section VII and the rest of them acted like children playing at secret service. They risked precious air time, and gave the British monitoring services some more opportunity to eavesdrop, to pass a tip that was utterly valueless.

Then a new thought made Grau frown. He knew about Le Petit Club all right – but how had Section VII found out? This was the kind of local knowledge he hoarded, just in case it might be useful one day, but never passed on.

So who had told Section VII?

Of course there were other agents around, but Grau had a good suspicion not that many. In any case, he hated the idea that he was competing with an unknown colleague, like another commercial traveller trying to sell the same goods to the same clients. If the department had managed to instal so many people, it should spread their efforts around.

And Reinecke and his crowd should trust him sufficiently not to give him obvious information which he already knew.

Yes, above all things they should trust him.

15

With the travel warrant, Ince gave Loach a sealed envelope marked OHMS and addressed to the commanding officer.

'It's our special training establishment,' said Ince. 'You'll get a full briefing when you get there.'

'Inverloch?' said Loach, as if repeating the name would explain a lot more.

'It's quite isolated,' said Ince. 'Has to be. We don't want anybody snooping around.'

'I thought that I was going operational,' said Loach. 'You said the other business...'

'I know what I said,' said Ince, crisply. 'And you are going operational. You're going to Inverloch.'

'For training?'

'Very special training...'

'But I've been through all that.'

'Not what they do here,' said Ince. 'It's something rather different.'

He lowered his voice.

'As a matter of fact, only people with special clearance can go.'

There was a knock at the door, and the colonel came in. They stood up.

The colonel nodded to Loach.

'Just off, are you?'

'Yes, sir,' said Loach.

'You'll find it very interesting,' said the colonel.

Loach looked at him blankly.

'I thought I was going to France, sir.'

'This came right from the top, Loach. Special orders.'

Ince looked at his watch.

'You'll get to King's Cross in good time,' he said. 'And a car will meet you at the other end.'

Loach thought they were anxious to get rid of him.

'I am staying in the Section, am I not? I mean, this isn't a transfer?' he said, and his voice sounded a little worried.

'Inverloch *is* the Section,' said Ince.

'Maybe the most interesting part,' said the colonel.

'That's why nobody knows much about it,' said Ince.

It was only when he settled back in his first-class reserved seat on the night train that Loach realized he still didn't know a thing about Inverloch.

Clare

16

It was the third step on the second flight she had to be careful about. That was the one that creaked, and set off some kind of alarm.

She tensed herself as she went up the stairs, counting the steps, placing her foot gently, and holding her pistol, ready to fire.

They called the house the Rat Run, and if you failed it, you were set back on the course, and were exposed to an extra dose of Maguire's sarcasm.

Maguire was Clare's conducting officer, and they said that in civilian life he was a history don at Oxford. He had also made four trips across the Channel for F Section, and lost two fingers on his right hand. Now he was handling the new intake, and Clare was sure he disliked her.

No matter what, she wasn't going to give him the satisfaction of seeing her fail.

Basically, the Rat Run was simply a test in housebreaking. They had to break in, by the back door, or through the french windows, or what other way they chose, each in turn, and then explore the place, from cellar to attic, opening doors, feeling their way along narrow passages and down corridors, across landings.

And, at any second, they had to be ready to shoot to kill.

If they triggered an alarm, stumbled across a trip-wire, set off a warning bell or a flashing light, they lost.

And so they did if they killed the wrong person. For anywhere in the house, dummy figures were liable to suddenly jump out at one, drop from a ceiling, appear round a corner.

If the dummy wore German uniform, and you shot to kill, that meant a point. But if he was in battledress, or had a beret, and you fired, that was a black mark.

The trouble was, you only had a fleeting second to decide,

and pull the trigger. Reynolds, the French-Canadian, had shot a nun three times in the breast. She was a special trick dummy, the pride and joy of Maguire and his kind, and she suddenly appeared behind a door. Reynolds didn't hesitate, and fired.

Clare reached the top of the landing, and turned right towards the window—

Crack!

She fired, instinctively.

The dummy grinned at her inanely, its dead eyes staring straight ahead.

Carefully, Clare approached, gun still held ready.

'Never think they're dead just because they look it,' Nelson, the weapons instructor, told her.

Not even if they're a dummy.

She had shot well, and if he had been flesh and blood, the dummy would have been very dead.

Which was just as well, since he wore the uniform of a Wehrmacht *hauptmann*.

The dummy had dropped from a trapdoor in the ceiling, and Clare wondered if it was chance, or somebody released these little surprises one by one. Maybe somebody was watching, finger poised on the button that would release the next surprise...

All she wanted was to find the envelope and then get out of the place.

The envelope, so said Maguire, was on a dressing-table in the master bedroom.

'It's quite simple, really,' he sneered. 'You break in, you go upstairs, you kill any German you bump into, you try not to kill your own people, you find the envelope, and bring it to me. And be quick about it.'

The door in front of her was ajar, and Clare was about to push it open. Then, instinct warned her. It seemed too simple, too easy.

She tried to peer into the room beyond the door, but it was dark and she had difficulty in seeing. Carefully she shone the beam from her torch through the gap. Torches had to be used with caution. In a dark house, the roving beam of a torch can arouse the curiosity of a passing policeman in the street outside...

What the torch lit up was enough to make Clare realize she was wise not to enter. There was no floor to the room – just a big yawning opening. If she had stepped into it, she would have fallen through.

It wouldn't do her much harm. There'd be a mattress to cushion her fall. But Maguire would say mockingly, 'Well done, Miss Gilbert – if this was the real thing, you'd be stuck with two broken legs in the cellar of a house until they find you.'

Clare stepped back. Not this time, friend. She turned, and went towards the other door, the closed one – just as, from behind a wardrobe, a hand appeared.

Clare's finger tightened on the trigger, then momentarily, she hesitated. Just as well, because the hand belonged to the dummy figure of a small child, a grotesque, stunted dwarf.

She opened the closed door, and found herself in the bedroom. And there, in front of the mirror on the dressing-table, was the envelope.

The room seemed safe enough, the bed neatly made, the covers turned back, ready for the occupants. Strangely, the room was also well furnished. A soft carpet, a nice lamp, even an oil painting on the wall.

She crossed to the dressing-table, and picked up the envelope. It was sealed. She tucked it into her battledress blouse, and left.

As she did so, the lamp crashed down.

Clare froze.

Nobody was there. The house was completely silent. Only her breathing, try as she would, could not keep still.

After that, she made her way out as quickly as possible, along the corridor, down the two flights of stairs, missing the third step from the bottom on the second one.

In the hall, she was sure that she had cleared the course. She was sure until the figure of the man in the leather coat shot up in front of her, hand outstretched.

Clare had tucked her pistol into the waistband of her battle-dress. She made a grab for it – and the figure moved, towards her.

This was no dummy. This was no creature of painted canvas and sawdust hanging from a trapdoor by wires. This was alive.

The lights went on.

It was Maguire.

'We're not all dummies here, Miss Gilbert,' he said. He held out his hand for the envelope.

'I didn't know anybody would be real,' she gasped. 'If I had shot . . .'

Maguire took the envelope.

'It's just as well you didn't then, isn't it?' he said.

They left the Rat Run by the front door.

'That'll be all for tonight,' said Maguire. 'Be ready at 0700 hours.'

'Yes, sir,' said Clare. 'I'll just turn in the gun.'

Maguire nodded.

She had started to walk away when he called after her.

'Oh, Miss Gilbert.'

'Sir?'

'That third step on the second flight of stairs. It doesn't make any noise at all.'

17

Sadler was the expert on silent killing.

He took over where the pistol and the sub-machine-gun left off. In his hands, a nail file, a steel comb, a length of thin wire were deadly. And the hands themselves were the most lethal.

Sadler enjoyed training women in his methods. He coached

them in the most savage form of unarmed combat with loving care.

The instructors at Ferny Bank were a mixed lot. Some had been seconded from Scotland Yard. Their speciality were skills like concealing a roll of microfilm in places of the body only a medical student would dream about. Some of the radio instructors were Royal Navy petty officers, to whom Morse was a symphony. There was a sergeant who had done three years in Pentonville for safebreaking, and now was coaching a class in that craft. And the civilian who showed them how to steal a car without having the ignition key did not have purely theoretical knowledge of that activity.

Sadler was something special. Rumour had it that he had been a member of the Hong Kong police, and that it was in the Far East he learnt the intricacies of his hobby.

For killing with bare hands, or using such harmless objects as propelling pencils or umbrellas to murder someone seemed to be more of a hobby with him than a grim knowledge obtained as part of his duties.

Clare was one of his great successes. She came on the course a nice, well-brought-up young lady. But in her was an ugly temper, and Sadler soon spotted a streak of ferocity that could be most useful.

Not that Sadler put the emphasis on killing.

'I want you to incapacitate your opponent,' he said with relish. At her first session, he looked at Clare and asked:

'Tell me, if some bastard grabbed you on a dark night in an alley and tried to rape you, what would you do, Miss?'

'Kick him in the balls,' said Clare sweetly.

After that, she and Sadler got on famously.

There were other women on the course, and Sadler liked to match them against each other.

'Now we're not going to have any fist fights, ladies,' he would say, as two girls faced each other nervously. 'It would be a pity if you damaged your knuckles.'

And everybody laughed, except the two girls.

'Use the heel of your open hand,' Sadler urged. 'Use leverage. Leverage is the secret – and where to hurt.'

And he would call out to Clare to come forward and show how it's done.

'Remember that a woman is just as deadly as a man,' Sadler said. 'She can pull a trigger as easily, stick a knife in a back just as well as a man – and when it comes to bashing his skull in, you'd be surprised how good a lady can be.'

After that he would set one of the girls to throw a man from behind, or strike at a nerve on the neck which would finish her opponent.

'Beautiful,' he told Clare after one exercise. 'You can use a knife like an artist uses his paint brush.'

Sometimes he would sermonize on the philosophy of his deadly subject.

'Don't think of it as killing. In fact, I don't ever want you to kill a German if you can help it. Put him out of action. But keep him alive. He is more use half-alive than completely dead. He still has to be looked after. He needs nurses, doctors, a hospital bed, manpower. He wastes their resources. Put him away for a year. Mash his balls so he can't breed any little Hitlers – or give his fraulein much joy. Cripple the bastard, but keep him alive.'

He followed this with a graphic demonstration of how a man's eye can be put out with the end of an umbrella.

Clare wasn't a bad shot, but Sadler dismissed marksmanship as more of an indulgence.

'I'm talking about keeping you alive,' he said. 'It's all very well them teaching you how to use Brens and Stens and bazookas and piats, but when the time comes you aren't going to have an arsenal handy. Chances are your gun is in the attic, and all you've got are your hands. And maybe your nylons. Great for strangling, nylons.'

She didn't admit to anyone, but Clare enjoyed learning to become a killer. It was not all the feeling of confidence it gave her, to know that despite her size she could tackle somebody twice as big and heavy. She actually liked the feeling of mastery in a tussle.

There was Margit, a Polish girl, and several times Clare was pitched against her. Clare liked the triumph she felt when Margit flew over her shoulder, or she had the brunette in an agonizing arm hold. And when Margit, panting, annoyed, reacted, and it was girl against girl, in a kind of mock duel, Clare enjoyed the satisfaction of bringing her to her knees.

'You must never let it get personal,' said Sadler. 'You've got to be like a doctor, operating on a patient. Never hate the person you're going to kill. You might botch it up.'

18

This morning, Sadler took Clare and her group through a brief unarmed combat session, and then sent them off to breakfast.

In the cafeteria, with the french windows overlooking the lawn, she stood in line with her tray, and collected her breakfast – reconstituted powdered egg, a slice of toast, a dab of margarine, some jelly-like marmalade, and tea.

Clare liked meals in the cafeteria, because they were one of the few times she managed to get a glimpse of her colleagues. They were all split up into different groups, and only met by chance, if they happened to join in the same training session.

The people here were all kinds, men and women, some quite young, some older, some with a trace of accent, others speaking perfect English.

They had only one thing in common – all of them were being trained to become secret agents. All of them knew that one night, perhaps quite soon, a black- or silver-painted Lysander would set them down in a field in France or Holland, or they would drop by parachute, or, perhaps, come ashore in a boat on enemy territory.

Clare had never established a relationship with any of them.

And it wasn't encouraged. The less they all knew about each other, the better.

She wasn't even quite sure what she was being trained for. She guessed it might be a courier, or perhaps they had her earmarked as a pianist – a radio operator, then again it could be something special?

'May I sit here?' asked a voice, and, without waiting for her answer, the lieutenant with Royal Berkshire Regiment badges put down his tray opposite her.

He sat down, and looked at the yellow excuse for scrambled egg with disgust.

'I think this is all part of it,' he said.

'Part of what?' asked Clare, studying him.

'Trying to break our spirit,' he said. 'If we can take this stuff, we can cope with anything.'

'Oh,' she said. She wasn't very interested.

'You can tell what they've got in store for you from the kind of breakfast you get,' he said.

'How?'

'Easy. A real egg and one rasher of bacon, you're going on a mission. Two real eggs, fried bread, and two rashers, it's a dicey one. Three eggs, you never come back.'

'And powdered egg?'

'Us,' he said. 'Boyscout stuff.'

'Excuse me,' Clare said, getting ready to leave.

'Oh, don't go yet,' he said.

She looked at her wristwatch.

'I'm due in . . .'

'Your Q-code test doesn't start for half an hour,' he said.

She was surprised. He wasn't part of her group.

'I have to get ready,' she said, wondering how he knew her schedule.

'You're with Maguire, aren't you?' he said.

The first thing they had told her was 'need to know'. If somebody didn't need to know, don't tell them. He seemed to know, but should he . . .

'It's all right,' he said. 'My name is Martin.'

As if that explained it.

'I'm Clare,' she said.

He nodded approvingly.

'Well done, no second names. You *have* learnt the book.'

'I'm sorry,' said Clare. 'I mean, I know we're all right here – but they did say we should . . .'

'Don't apologize,' said the lieutenant. 'Major Ince will approve.'

'Major Ince?'

'Oh, don't you know our Major Ince? He of the thin smile.'

Clare shook her head.

'I don't think so,' she said.

'I wouldn't worry,' he said. 'He's bound to know you, even if you don't know him.'

That worried Clare a little.

'What does he do?' she asked.

'He's around,' said the lieutenant vaguely.

He had finished his breakfast, lit a cigarette. He didn't offer Clare one.

He saw her face.

'Oh, I'm sorry,' he said, offering her his pack. 'I thought you didn't smoke.'

'I don't, thanks,' she said.

But she wondered, how the hell does he know.

'Do you ever get up to town?' he asked.

'They don't give me much time off in this place,' said Clare.

'Well, when you do, let's have dinner,' said the lieutenant. There was no question in his voice.

'They don't encourage that here,' said Clare.

'They need never know, need they?'

And his eyes stared straight into hers.

'Fraternizing isn't encouraged,' said Clare.

She stood up.

'See you soon,' said the lieutenant. He watched her excellent figure as she moved off between the tables.

Actually, he'd rather enjoy taking that one out.
And not just because he was a security officer.

19

They had strung up an aerial wire between two branches, and now Clare sat, earphones on her head, hunched over the compact field Morse transmitter which actually looked like a suitcase.

The Royal Navy petty officer watched her closely.

'Accept my priority message at once,' he snapped.

'QTP,' tapped Clare.

'Send for sixty seconds,' said the petty officer, looking at his stop-watch.

'QTP,' tapped Clare. 'QTP.'

The petty officer timed her.

Back through the earphones came the signal:

'QRV ... QRV ... QRV ...'

'Well?' said the petty officer.

Clare nodded.

'They are ready.'

'Go ahead,' he said. 'Start sending it ...'

Clare began tapping out the test message she had herself carefully encoded in its groups of four letters split up into sixteen sections.

Suddenly the petty officer raised his hand.

'Stop,' he barked.

Clare, finger on the morse key, froze.

'Emergency,' said the petty officer. 'The boche is round the corner.'

'I have to finish the message,' said Clare.

'It's too late,' he said.

Clare hesitated.

'Well, don't leave them high and dry,' said the petty officer. 'Break off.'

'QTR,' flashed Clare urgently. 'QTR, QTR . . .'

It was the most ominous code signal of them all: 'I must stop. Imminent danger. I will try to contact you again.'

'If you send QTR,' Maguire had told his group once, 'you're in deep trouble. It's the last message most operators manage to get out before they've had it.'

Rumour had it that it was on the mission that Maguire sent his own QTR signal that he had lost his two fingers.

But what happened in that back room the night the German direction-finders pin-pointed him was something that remained a mystery to the group.

'Right,' said the petty officer, 'pack it in.'

Clare tore off her headphones, unlocked the aerial on the tree, and while the petty officer timed her, packed the suitcase . . .

'You're still taking too long,' said the petty officer. 'By now you're supposed to be cycling away.'

'I'd never make it,' said Clare.

'I wouldn't bother then,' said the petty officer unfeelingly. 'Just shoot yourself.'

She had now had six weeks of it, lectures, tests, briefings, small arms, assembling a machine gun in the dark, unarmed combat, radio work.

Like the sabotage session that followed the Q-test that day.

'This is a beautiful invention,' said the lecturer, lovingly displaying what looked like a bit of dark-brown dough. 'Basically it's cyclonite, ladies and gentlemen, and it's a dream.'

He weighed the lump in his hand, and then suddenly threw it across the room.

'Here, catch,' he said, and one of them, sitting next to Clare, managed to capture the ball of dough, white-faced.

'Quite safe, it really is quite safe,' beamed the lecturer. 'You can blow up anything with it, but it doesn't matter if you drop it, or squeeze it, or sit on it, or fire a bullet into it. It's insensitive.'

The plasticine-like mass had an almond smell, and the lecturer said casually:

'Of course, I wouldn't sniff it for too long. Might give you a nasty headache.'

Later that morning, Clare was walking down the corridor when Maguire stopped her.

'You're doing quite nicely,' he said. 'The practical results are good.'

'Thank you, sir,' she said. This was not like the usual Maguire.

'You've been going at it without a break,' he said. 'So I'm giving you twenty-four hours' leave. Go to London. Get away from this place.'

'I'd rather carry on, sir,' she said. 'I want to get the field test over.'

'Change of air will do you good,' said Maguire. 'And the boyfriend will appreciate it.'

Clare's face was expressionless.

'You do have a boyfriend, don't you?'

'I never know when I can see him,' she said vaguely. 'He's an American.'

'Well, give him a call and tell him you're on your way. See you in twenty-four hours.'

20

Grau pressed the second-floor button, and didn't feel anything was wrong as the lift went up. But as soon as he unlocked the door, and entered the flat, he sensed trouble. His instinct alerted him before he knew the reason.

He went across the corridor to his room, but before he could enter, Mrs Croxley opened her living-room door and called out to him.

'Mr Harris, I've got a surprise for you.'

Christ, thought Grau. What's gone wrong. Police? Some check up?

'Do come in,' said Mrs Croxley, and he saw now that she was wearing her Sunday dress. Only it wasn't Sunday.

'Jimmy's here,' said Mrs Croxley proudly, and stood aside to let him enter the room.

Ah, the prodigal son in the RAF. Grau made a suitable smile as he faced the boy. He was lean and lanky, and had light-blond eyelashes, something Grau hated. He had taken off his RAF tunic, but he still had on his uniform trousers, suspended by braces over the blue shirt. The tie was off.

'Pleased to meet you,' said Jimmy, without getting up.

'Your mother has told me a lot about you,' said Grau. All he wanted was to leave the two of them to it.

'Mr Harris is a very nice gentleman,' said Mrs Croxley, as if trying to justify Grau's acceptance as her lodger.

'What do you do, Mr Harris?' asked Jimmy.

'Mr Harris runs a bookshop, don't you, Mr Harris?' said Mrs Croxley.

'Second-hand books,' muttered Grau.

Jimmy sniffed.

'Not much money in that, I should have thought.'

'Ah, people read a lot these days,' said Grau. 'Not much else they can do in the blackout, is there?'

'Oh, I don't know,' leered Jimmy.

Grau now knew that he not only disliked young Croxley, he hated him. He hoped he'd fall down the lift-shaft and break his neck.

And why shouldn't he be asking him questions?

'How's the Air Force?' said Grau.

'Busy,' said Jimmy.

'He's in Bomber Command,' said Mrs Croxley proudly.

'You mustn't talk about that, Mum.'

Stupid bastard, thought Grau. Trying to make himself important. I'll show him.

'Ground crew, aren't you?' said Grau.

Jimmy looked at her reproachfully.

'You've been doing careless talk, Mum, I told you not to.'

'Mr Harris is all right,' said Mrs Croxley, giving her lodger a warm look. 'I'll make us some tea.'

She bustled into the kitchen.

I've got to get out of this, thought Grau. I'll say I am going somewhere, anything. Only I can't spend the evening here with this woman and her son.

Jimmy sniffed.

'Where do you come from, Mr Harris?' he asked.

Every alarm bell jangled in Grau's head.

'London's my home,' he said.

'Oh yes?' said Jimmy.

Did he seem unconvinced? I must head him off, decided Grau.

'How long are you home for?' asked Grau.

'I got twenty-four hours,' said Jimmy.

'That's not very much – I thought the least they'd give people is seventy-two hours.'

Jimmy sniffed.

'We're very busy.'

'Is it a long journey?'

'Four hours,' said Jimmy.

'Of course I mustn't ask you where,' said Grau.

'That's right,' said Jimmy.

'Are you men getting to know each other?' trilled Mrs Croxley from the kitchen.

'Jimmy and I are getting on fine,' called back Grau. 'Aren't we, Jimmy?'

'That's right,' sniffed Jimmy. He got out a Woodbine and lit it. He didn't ask Grau if he smoked.

'Do you do anything, in the war,' said Jimmy suddenly.

'I'm afraid I'm just a civilian,' said Grau.

'Not even Civil Defence?'

'We don't get many air raids these days, do we?'

Jimmy gave a pimply smile.

'No, it's our turn to show Schiklgruber.'

He scratched himself.

'I didn't know bookshops was a reserved occupation,' said Jimmy.

God almighty, thought Grau. When is he going to stop interrogating me.

'They're not, that's why we can't get anybody.'

'Didn't you get called up?' asked Jimmy.

'Flat feet,' said Grau.

Mrs Croxley came in with the tea.

'Chocolate biscuits,' she announced proudly. 'I saved some points specially.'

Jimmy slurped his tea.

Grau didn't know how he sat through it, but he had a second cup and agreed with every word Mrs Croxley said and approved of everything Jimmy did, and was all interested in the boy, most considerate of his mother and counting every minute.

Finally, he excused himself.

'Oh, what a pity, Mr Harris,' said Mrs Croxley. 'I thought we could have a cosy little evening.'

'I'm sorry,' said Grau. 'I have to see somebody – about buying some old books.'

'All work and no play,' said Jimmy and gave a reedy cackle.

'I wish I hadn't arranged it with him,' said Grau.

He could hardly wait to get into the blackout.

'I don't like that bloke,' said Jimmy, after Grau had gone.

'Mr Harris? He's ever so nice. And no trouble at all. I couldn't have a better lodger,' said Mrs Croxley.

'Don't like him, Mum.'

'Whatever is the matter with him? You know how useful the money is.'

'I know, Mum,' said Jimmy. 'I just don't trust him.'

21

Her father suggested meeting at the Savoy at seven, in the cocktail bar. Clare wondered why she had phoned him at all. She didn't really want to see him, and yet she knew as soon as she got off the train that she would call him.

'I've got some leave, Daddy,' she said.

'You should have let me know,' he said reproachfully. 'How long are you down for.'

'Only today,' she said.

'They must owe you at least a week,' he said. 'Where are you now?'

'At the station.'

'And you go back . . .?'

'Tomorrow morning.'

'Damn,' he said. 'All right, never mind. We'll have dinner tonight.'

After she put the receiver down, she wondered why she bothered. They hadn't seen each other for nearly two months. And she honestly didn't mind. The fact that she was hidden away in the country was a wonderful excuse.

It had been like that ever since her mother left, a year before the war. Clare was away at her posh school and it was left until her summer holidays for her to find out that her parents had broken up.

Clare's mother was French, vivacious, dark-eyed, and beautiful, and Clare adored her. When she first started thinking about these things, she couldn't work out what made her mother marry her father in the first place.

And yet, between father and daughter, there was a curious bond, a kind of mutual respect which often demonstrated itself, quite irrationally, in temperamental flare-ups and rows.

Clare was about twelve when she first suspected that all was not well between her parents. She would always remember the night she stood shivering in the corridor of the smart flat off Sloane Street and, through their bedroom door, heard the awful quarrel, the first of many.

At breakfast, they were both perfectly polite and correct to one another, obviously keeping up a front. Clare's eyes darted furtively from one to the other over the toast and tea, trying to find a clue, an explanation for what had gone on between them during the night.

But in front of Clare, like a temporary truce in a civil war, they took care to keep appearances normal.

Clare felt like screaming at them.

'Don't play-act,' she wanted to shout. 'Don't treat me like an idiot. I know there's no Santa Claus. I don't believe in fairy stories. And I know you row like fury. If only you'd tell me what's wrong. Maybe I could help. But at least give me credit for knowing what's going on.'

But her mother smiled sweetly at her, and her father gave her a peck on the cheek when he left for the office.

She had no idea what was wrong between them. She knew they had met in Salzburg, on some winter holiday, the elegant, attractive French girl and the English businessman, that they got married soon after at Caxton Hall. There was some religious problem, her mother was Catholic, her father couldn't care less but called himself Church of England.

Clare went over to France every year, and met her grandma. And she couldn't remember a time when she didn't speak French as fluently as English.

When the break-up came, they took her out to tea to explain it to her. Clare often wondered afterwards why they had to make an event of it. Perhaps they wanted to do it on neutral ground.

Her mother explained that, of course, they both loved her, and they would continue to be her father and mother, and she would of course come over to France to spend the summer holidays with Mother, but she'd live the rest of the year with Daddy.

'We mustn't uproot you, darling,' they said. 'You're getting on so well at school, and you're a boarder anyway, so it doesn't make any difference really does it?'

'Are you getting divorced?' asked Clare, biting into a chocolate eclair, but her big eyes very alert.

'Nothing like that,' said her father. 'We have merely decided to separate for a little while. We'll still be very much married.'

It didn't seem a very logical remark, but Clare was much too confused and puzzled and worried to work it out.

'I'll always be there when you need me, sweetie,' said her mother.

'You know you're the most important thing in the world to us,' said her father.

And Clare wanted to ask why, if they could agree on that, they couldn't just stick together, but then the waitress came with some more hot water for the tea, and the moment passed.

When she was home from school, her father gave her everything she wanted, spoiled her shamelessly, but was seldom around to be with her.

And when she went over to France, and stayed with her mother, her father was never mentioned. But it was a lovely holiday, that beautiful summer of 1939, and Clare was quite happy.

The terrible moment came one evening in the flat in Knightsbridge, after she returned to London.

Clare knew, vaguely, that her father had been seeing some woman or other, somebody called Margaret, and she had come over to dinner once. Clare thought she was all right, and they were both on their most correct social Emily Post routine in front of the girl.

'I think your daughter is sweet,' said Margaret, and Clare didn't particularly like her for that.

But then came the evening when Clare wanted to show her father a little necklace mother had given her in Paris, and she went unannounced into the lounge and there stood father and Margaret in a close, passionate embrace and it was the kind of kiss that Clare had never before seen.

She stood there, just staring at them.

'Oh, come in, dear,' said her father, disengaging himself a little awkwardly.

'Hallo, Clare,' said Margaret, hurriedly patting her hair.

Clare ignored her. But she stared at her father, unbelieving.

She felt tears in her eyes, and without a word she turned, and fled. She ran into her room, and slammed the door.

Her father tapped on the door, very gently.

'Clare,' he said softly.

She lay on the bed sobbing.

'May I come in, dear?' said her father.

'Go away,' she shouted.

Soon after, her father and Margaret left the flat for the evening, and Clare went to bed without even touching the food that was ready for her.

Looking back on it, she often thought that she behaved like a stupid little prig. Margaret was very nice, really, and her father and mother had split up, and why should she mind if he kissed his girlfriend?

Only it wasn't just a kiss, and Clare knew what else was going on between them as clearly as if she had walked into the bedroom and pulled the sheet away from their naked bodies, locked in each other.

She knew it was stupid and childish and immature, but at that moment she felt that her father had besmirched and fouled her mother by touching another woman.

And from that moment, whatever affection and need there was in her for her father, there was also hate.

22

He stood as she came to him, and kissed her on the cheek.

'Not in uniform?' he said, looking at her little costume.

'We don't wear it much,' she said.

He ordered a gin and tonic for her.

Just what was she doing had become a point of friction between them.

'How's the job?' he asked.

'All right,' she said.

'Still in the same place?'

She nodded. They had had an almighty blow-up about that. She told him that he could only write to her at 'Box 620, care of GPO, London'.

'Damn it, you're my own daughter,' he exploded. 'Do they think I'm going to betray you to the Germans? What's your proper address?'

'I'm sorry, Daddy,' Clare had said. 'That's all I'm allowed to give.'

'But where the hell is it?'

'Not far from London,' she said.

'Doing what?'

'Please, you mustn't ask me, really you mustn't.'

'I thought you replied to an advertisement for "multi-lingual secretaries".'

'I did,' she said. 'And then I had this selection board at the War Office, and you know the rest.'

'I don't know a damn thing,' he said. 'You joined the Army, I suppose.'

She nodded.

'You know, I could get annoyed,' he said. 'I handle more secret stuff in Berkeley Square in one day than you'll see in the whole war.'

Her father did something in the Ministry of Economic Warfare, and she knew it must be something important because they had even flown him to Washington twice.

'Daddy,' she said, 'you're ten times more important than I am, but I don't want to get into trouble.'

He snorted. Then, rather like the sun emerging after a squall, he relaxed.

'Well, how are you?'

'Fine,' she smiled. 'Fit as a fiddle.'

Then she asked the question.

'Heard anything from Mummy?'

'She's all right,' he said. 'I had a card through the Red Cross.'

Her mother had stayed in France when war was declared. Nobody then thought Paris was less secure than London. After all, London didn't even have a Maginot line.

'I must look after Grandma,' she had explained to Clare. 'She won't let herself be uprooted to England, and I'm quite all right here.'

Paris fell, and for three awful months there was no news.

Clare had nightmares of her mother being interned, shifted to some prison camp, made to do forced labour in a war factory. But, although she had married an Englishman, she was French, and the German Army had bigger things to do than to worry about an old woman being looked after by her daughter.

And it was through the Red Cross that they eventually heard everything was well.

'Can't we write to her?' asked Clare.

'No letters,' said her father. 'They're very strict about that. Especially in my work ...'

She thought, if you but knew ...

'Hungry?' he asked.

She nodded.

'Let's go,' he said.

They went through to the grill-room, the waiter switching on his welcoming smile.

'Good evening, Mr Gilbert,' he said, and pulled back the chair for Clare.

How often does he come here? wondered Clare, glancing at her father over the menu. Maybe always for dinner?

With Margaret?

She didn't know why she even broached the subject, but she asked:

'How's Margaret?'

Her father, who took most things in his stride, looked surprised. After the incident in the flat, they had never discussed her. A couple of days after that evening, he had tried, very gently, to talk to Clare about it, but she had merely said, 'That's all right, Daddy. No need for explanations.'

'But I want you to understand ...'

'Please, Daddy, I'd rather not talk about it.'

'Clare, you're being rather silly. I know how you feel about your mother, but you must understand . . .'

'Please,' she had pleaded.

It left nothing more to be said, and that was the last time father and daughter had mentioned it.

And now, out of the blue, she came up with the name.

'Margaret? Oh, she's fine.'

'That's nice,' said Clare, impersonally.

'She's working at Bush House.'

'Oh?' said Clare.

'She's very good at languages,' said her father.

'I didn't know.'

Her father was no coward.

'Why did you ask?'

Clare gave a slight shrug.

'Just curious,' she said lightly. 'I imagine you've been seeing a lot of her.'

'She's a very nice person,' he said.

'I'm sure,' said Clare. She hoped it didn't sound sarcastic. She was trying hard not to be a bitch.

The head waiter appeared, and they ordered, a one-star starter, and a two-star main course.

Then her father picked the wine, and Clare wondered what they'd talk about for the rest of the meal. Actually, that wasn't fair. She liked him as a person. She wasn't so sure she liked him as a father.

'Tell me,' he said, 'how would you feel – if I married her?'

Clare controlled her voice.

'Are you going to?'

'Well, not till the war's over, of course. Your mother and I are still married, and we can't do anything about that at the moment. Not with her over there.'

Clare thought nastily, what a bore for you. How inconvenient the war must be for you and Margaret.

'But you're going to?'

'Oh, I don't know. Who can make plans these days?'

Clare asked, 'What does she do at Bush House?'

'She's something in the monitoring service.'

'With the BBC?'

'Sort of.'

The waiter brought the soup, and that's all they discussed about Margaret.

And Clare never asked the questions she would have liked to, but never could have. Like, do you sleep with her a lot? Do you often come here for dinner? Sit at this table? Maybe the waiters look at me, and think you're ringing the changes – I'm a new attraction.

The food was good, especially after the kind of cooking she'd been having.

Over the meal, her father was amusing, considerate, just the right dinner companion. He knew when to concentrate on eating, and when to break the silence with a little chat.

'Have you seen that film yet?' he asked when the sweet came.

'The Chaplin one? *The Great Dictator*?'

'No,' he said. 'The one about security. *Next of Kin*.'

'Haven't had time yet,' she said.

'I should have thought you would have been made to go,' he said. 'It was supposed to be a training film in the first place. It's very good.'

'Sounds a real Ministry of Information epic,' she said. 'I'd rather see *Gone With the Wind*.'

'It's a bit frightening,' he said. 'How somebody's always listening, picking up scraps of information. Brings it home to people how dangerous careless talk can be.'

She laughed.

'Now you know why I can't give you my address.'

'Don't start again, Clare. You know what I mean.'

'Anyway, not at the Savoy, I hope,' she smiled.

She looked around at the discreetly lit room, the uniforms, the women determined to look their best despite clothes rationing, the American war correspondents – and then she saw him.

The lieutenant with Royal Berkshire Regiment badges.

He was sitting with a WREN three or four tables away, and when her eyes caught him, he was already studying her. As soon as he saw that she had spotted him, he nodded and smiled.

Her father noticed it.

'Somebody you know?'

'I had breakfast with him,' she said.

'You know him that well?'

'Don't be stupid,' she said. 'We shared a table in the cafeteria.'

'Oh, you work with him?'

'He happened to be there.'

To her surprise, the lieutenant said something to the girl with him, stood up, and came over to their table.

'Hallo, Clare,' he said. 'This is a nice surprise.'

'It is, Martin,' she said, rather cool.

He looked at her father.

'This is my dad,' said Clare, feeling a little schoolgirlish.

'A pleasure, Mr Gilbert,' said the lieutenant.

So he did know the name.

'Please join us,' said her father. 'Perhaps you and your companion . . .'

'That's awfully kind, sir,' the lieutenant said, in best public school manner, 'but we're going on somewhere, and we're late already. Forgive my cheek for butting in like this – but it was so unexpected, seeing your daughter here . . .'

He smiled at Clare.

'Makes a change from powdered eggs, eh?'

'They just know how to make them better,' said her father lightly.

The lieutenant excused himself charmingly.

'Enjoy your leave,' he said to Clare. And, more formally to her father, 'Delighted to meet you, Mr Gilbert.'

He returned to his table, and the WREN gave them a sweet smile.

'Well, that was a coincidence,' said her father. 'Nice boy.'

'I suppose so,' said Clare.

By the time they had coffee, the lieutenant and the Navy girl had finished their dinner, and left. As they walked out, he gave Clare a cheery wave.

Her father followed them with his eyes.

'You know,' he said thoughtfully, 'I think I've seen that chap somewhere.'

'You sure?'

She was very alert now.

He nodded.

'Where on earth would you meet him?'

'He was with a man called Glover – that's it, he was with Glover ...'

'And who's Glover?' asked Clare.

'You wouldn't know him,' said her father. 'He's at the Ministry.'

'Your Ministry?'

'Yes,' said her father. 'He's a security man.'

23

Later that night she caught up with Tony in the officers' club in Park Lane. She explained to her father, as they emerged into the blacked-out Strand, that, really, she needed an early night.

'I've got to get a train back first thing in the morning,' she explained.

'I think it's ridiculous, giving you just a few hours,' said her father.

She gave a hasty, formal peck on the cheek.

'They can't run the war without me,' said Clare, lightly.

'When do I see you?'

Probably just before they drop me in France, she thought.

But all she said was: 'Soon.'

'I'll take you in a cab,' he said. 'Where are staying?'

'A sort of hostel – but don't bother. I'll walk. It's quite near.'

'Trying to get rid of me?'

'I'd like a bit of fresh air. Gives me a chance to see some shops,' said Clare.

'In the blackout?' He snorted.

Oh, how the hell do I shake him off?

'You can't walk by yourself,' he said. 'Not all alone.'

I can kill people, she felt like saying. I can make them die quite quickly with a hat needle, or a bit of wire. I can break their arm. Just stop fussing.

'Don't be silly,' said Clare. 'I'll be fine.'

She stole a side glance at her wristwatch. Tony would already be waiting at Willow Run.

'I think you've got a date,' he said. 'With a Pole. Or a GI.'

She smiled.

'See you soon, Daddy. And thanks for the dinner.'

She left him looking after her as she walked off with a wave.

Then, as soon as he had faded in the dark, she hailed a cruising cab.

'Grosvenor House,' she said.

Tony was a navigator on a B-24, based with his wing at Fakenham, in Norfolk. He was on his second tour of missions, and when he was drunk he always told her that he was living on borrowed time.

Maybe that was one reason she saw him from time to time. She felt secure. There could be no involvement here. He might not return from a raid. And if he always did, eventually he'd go home. Far away. Thousands of miles away, to far off Denver. It couldn't come to anything, and she liked it that way. It was less complicated.

She had the number at the base, and she called the orderly room. Yes, he had said, he could get to London that evening. See you at Willow Run. After you've ditched your old man.

And there he was, in his Eisenhower jacket, and his battered hat.

'You look great, honey,' he said, and kissed her.

He always said that. It seemed to be a kind of password, to be used on meeting a date. Tell them they look great, and after that it's all smooth going.

'Want a drink?'

She nodded.

He looked round the crowded lobby, the cool, antiseptic American Red Cross girls coping with all kinds of officers, tall, short, fat, thin, Air Corps, Infantry, just in, just leaving, just coming, just going.

'You'll have to share a room, Major.' 'Sorry, Lieutenant, no seats at the Palladium tomorrow.' 'Sure, we'll give you a call at six AM, Captain.' 'I'm sorry, sir, Miss Ridgeway didn't call, no message, Colonel.' 'You'll have to wear Class A uniform there, Lieutenant.'

'Jesus,' said Tony. 'Let's get out of here.'

He took her arm, and steered her round one corner and then another, into South Audley Street, and then along Curzon Street, and into Shepherd's Market, and the dimly lit club he called the joint.

He signed her in, and they found a couple of places, near a Canadian squadron leader who was telling a blonde with bulging breasts that baseball is the greatest game in the world.

Tony gave Clare an appreciative look.

'Gee, you're looking great,' he said.

'That's twice you've said it,' said Clare, without complaint.

'Couldn't we have had dinner?'

'I had to see my father,' said Clare.

'I thought you didn't get on,' said Tony.

'Oh, he's all right.'

'Anyway, it's lucky I could make it. We were on standby.'

'What happened?' asked Clare.

' "Sad Sack" blew a fuse or something.'

'Sad Sack' was his Liberator.

'I'm sorry,' said Clare. Then she realized what a stupid thing she'd said. 'No, I'm not. I'm glad.'

'But I got to leave early,' he said. 'They've got a busload of fellows going back first thing. Six AM.'

'Me too. If I don't get the early train, I'm for it.'

'So,' said Tony, looking at her intently. 'What do we do till then?'

She knew exactly what he meant.

'I'm pretty tired.'

'Hell, you can sleep all day tomorrow,' he said.

'Tomorrow, Captain, I have to be bright and alert, with all my wits around me.'

'Playing spook again, huh?'

'Just doing my job.'

'Where's your room?' asked Tony, direct as always.

'It's a service girls' hostel, and I'm sharing with three lady sergeants,' lied Clare.

'I don't mind,' said Tony.

'But they do mind.'

'OK,' he said. 'So we'll find ourselves a little place in darkest Paddington.'

I knew this would happen, thought Clare. And what can I tell him?

'Excuse me, Captain,' said the Canadian squadron leader, pronouncing each word very distinctly. 'Can I ask you a question, Captain?'

'Sure,' said Tony, his hand on Clare's knee. The blonde with the huge breasts gave Clare a cold, unfriendly look.

'Tell me, Captain, is baseball the greatest sport in the world? Tell the lady, Captain. What is the greatest sport in the world?'

Tony gave him a genial smile.

'Cricket,' he said, and turned back to Clare.

The Canadian squadron leader continued to give Tony an unbelieving look.

'Excuse me, Captain,' he said. 'Can I ask you another question?'

And he burped.

'Anything, buddy,' said Tony, his eyes on Clare's pale face.

'Are you an American, Captain?' asked the squadron leader. It took an effort.

'Yes, sir,' said Tony. 'Pure Apache.'

The squadron leader had lost interest, and his head drooped. The heavy-bosomed blonde shook him.

'Listen,' said Tony. 'I think we blow.'

'Already?' said Clare.

'Two's company,' said Tony. 'Let's go.'

Outside, in the dark, he took hold of her, and kissed her, hard.

'Now let's find that little room,' he said.

24

Clare did not enjoy the lovemaking. It was exactly what she couldn't tell him. They lay in bed, naked, and for her it was a mechanical exercise. That first time, months ago, it had seemed different. Now it seemed an unpleasant necessity.

She knew Tony, she knew his exploring hands and his seeking tongue, his eagerness to arouse her, and make her react to his desire. So far, each time they had been together, she had been able to convince him, and perhaps herself. But this night she lay rigid, unable to relax or to match his craving with any kind of warmth.

He squeezed her breasts, and played with her nipples, and forced himself into her. Her response was artificial, almost studied.

As he pressed on her, her eyes were open, staring at the ceiling. It was a rotten little room, in a fleapit hotel in Praed Street. The woman downstairs asked no questions. She was used to Americans who had missed the last train from Paddington, or were waiting for the first one, moving in for a few hours, and their only luggage was a woman. What passed for the hotel register was full of 'Mr and Mrs's' who often didn't even know each other's first names.

She hadn't even bothered to give Clare a curious look.

'We'll be leaving first thing in the morning,' Tony said.

'Room six, on the second floor,' she sniffed, pushing over the key. 'Fifteen bob.'

Tony paid her.

'You want tea?'

Tony looked at Clare, who shook her head.

'I'm sorry, honey,' said Tony when they got to the room. 'I know it's a dump . . .'

She kissed him then, out of kindness, not passion. She wanted to show him that she didn't mind, really she didn't. Not if it gave him what he wanted.

They arrived so late she had not seen anybody else, but she was sure the place was full, in each room a couple spending a few hours in each other's arms. As Tony fondled her, she was slightly nauseated at the thought of the same thing happening on either side of their thin walls, along the corridor, upstairs and downstairs. A kind of assembly line of sweating entangled couples on creaking mattresses, renting their coupling space at fifteen bob for a few hours.

Tony eased off her a little. He was far too nice to give her any hint of disappointment, or to make her feel embarrassed by her lack of wanting him.

So after his moment had come, he relaxed, and lay quietly, stroking her hair.

'I love you,' he said.

'Do you?'

He kissed her, and she was much relieved that having said the thing he felt was obligatory, he did not pursue the subject.

He sat up in bed, and reached over for a packet of PX cigarettes. He lit one.

'Say something French to me,' he said.

She stared at him, startled.

'Go on,' he said. 'I love to hear you talk French.'

'Don't be silly,' she said.

She'd once told him that her mother was French, and that she spoke it fluently. And he had laughed when she had said a few words.

'I wouldn't have believed you're English,' he had said. And she changed the conversation.

Now, unexpectedly, he came up with it again.

'You know what they should do,' he said. 'Drop you by parachute right on the Champs-Elysées so that you can sit all day in the Café de la Paix, listening to their careless talk. You'd be worth fifty spies.'

'I wouldn't be much good at it.'

'Nonsense,' he said. 'You look so innocent you'd fool old Himmler himself. The new Mata Hari.'

He laughed.

'Except that I know a secret or two about this Mata Hari,' he said, and traced a line along her naked breasts.

Then, suddenly:

'What the hell do you do all day anyway?'

She stiffened.

'I told you. It's sort of – secret.'

'No, I mean, what do *you* do? Pound a typewriter?'

'I'm a kind of secretary,' she lied.

'But why are you always so mysterious about it?'

'It's my boss,' she said. 'It's his work that's secret.'

'I bet,' said Tony. 'I bet he orders all the spam for Ike.'

She sat up on one elbow.

'Tony, how much time have we got?'

'Plenty,' he said.

'No, how much?'

'Two hours before my bus goes.'

'Let's go and have breakfast.'

'Now! In the middle of the night?'

'Please.'

He shook his head.

'I thought you were so tired...'

She looked round the room.

'I don't like this place.'

'It's me you're supposed to like,' he said, and reached for her.

But ten minutes later, they were getting dressed.

'Where the hell can you have breakfast in this town at four AM?' he grumbled, knotting his tie.

'I know,' she said. 'The Corner House.'

They walked past the reception desk, and the woman gave them an unblinking look. She couldn't quite make out Clare. The girl wasn't a prostitute, and she was really too high class to be taken for a quick one-night stand in Praed Street, and she wasn't the Yank's wife, and she wasn't a service girl because she didn't wear uniform, and as for the 'Capt and Mrs Brown' bit in the register, that was just a joke.

I wonder how much it cost him? she mused.

She settled back again, and was quite surprised when the door opened, and the blackout curtain rustled, and the man in the raincoat came in.

'You're out early, Sergeant,' she said.

'Making me rounds,' said Morris, who was a detective sergeant at Paddington Green. He was lying, and they both knew it.

'Got no deserters, spies, or black marketeers tonight,' said the woman, pushing the register towards him.

'Any foreigners?' he said.

'Free French matelot in number three.'

'With his missus.'

'Of course.'

Morris looked at the register almost disinterestedly.

'What about these two?' he asked, pointing at the last entry.

She leered.

'They left half an hour ago. A Yank and his piece.'

Morris nodded.

'Just came in for a quick warm-up, eh?'

'That's it,' she said. 'How about a cup of tea?'

'Not now,' he said. He put a folded sheet of paper on the counter. 'Watch out for these. Usual list of deserters in the district.'

'Of course. I'll call you if I get one.'

'Right.'

Outside, in the dark, an officer in uniform was waiting in the shadows.

'Well?' said the officer.

'Yes, sir,' said the detective sergeant from Paddington Green. 'Using the name Brown. Captain and Mrs Brown.'

The officer made a note on a small pad.

He was a lieutenant, with the insignia of the Royal Berkshire Regiment.

25

For Grau, the day was ruined at the corner of Baker Street and Marylebone Road when he bought a morning paper. At first he didn't notice it and then, just as he was about to turn the corner, he spotted a paragraph on the bottom of the front page.

'Spy Executed', was the headline, and Grau felt the tightening of the stomach muscles he dreaded, and the cold feeling of fear.

'A German spy, Jurgen Kronstadt, aged thirty-four, was hanged yesterday at Pentonville,' said the brief few lines. 'He was sentenced to death after a two-day trial held in camera at the Old Bailey last month.'

That was all.

Grau looked around furtively, as if half-expecting to see them descend on him from all sides. But of course, it all seemed normal. Nobody was staring at him. He was sure that nobody had been following him.

Across the road was a café, and Grau decided that he needed to sit down.

'Cup of tea,' he said to the waitress. He was really getting much too English, he thought to himself. A sudden shock, and the first thing he does is to rush for a cup of tea.

He looked at the paragraph again. The finality of it was

horrifying. Not 'spy sentenced'. Not 'spy arrested'. But 'spy executed'. Finished. That's the end of it.

The name Jurgen Kronstadt meant nothing to him. He had never heard of the fellow. He had no idea where he had been arrested. Or when.

Was he an AMT VII man? One of Reinecke's people?

As he sipped his tea, Grau studied the few lines of newsprint as if he could gradually prise the hidden facts out of the story. What worried him was the mention of a 'two-day' trial. That suggested the man, whoever he was, had pleaded not guilty. That suggested questions, interrogations, cross examinations. That meant they might have found out a lot.

On the other hand, why should it jeopardize him in any way? Just as he had never heard of Kronstadt, so presumably the man knew nothing of Grau.

So relax, my friend. They must have had this man Kronstadt in their hands for a long time, certainly weeks, maybe months. And nothing had happened. The fact that they had now executed him, and announced it publicly, would suggest that the file was closed.

Yet Grau felt uneasy. The man had been hanged. No officer? Not a military man behind the lines, but a civilian spy? Or did the British hang them all now, like criminals?

Grau, actually, was essentially pragmatic, and to him the important thing was not to be executed at all. Once it happened, it really didn't matter to him whether he was shot in the Tower, or hanged in a common prison, except that Grau had a sneaking suspicion that, maybe, shooting was more efficient.

He wondered how they caught this man Kronstadt? In the act of sending a Morse message from some back room? Or tramping along a beach after landing from a U-boat? Or passing forged money, proving yet once again that Hartmann and his false paper experts were not quite as brilliant as they thought?

It was cunning of the British to reveal so much and no more. Wryly, Grau thought that if the whole thing was intended to make people like himself jittery, it could not have done any better.

Grau wondered if other papers had more details. He rushed out of the café, across to Baker Street station and bought every daily paper. Then he sat on a bench in the station, and looked through them quickly.

Somewhere, they all had the item, and it always said the same thing, no more, and no less. But here, in the *Daily Telegraph*, there was something new.

'Kronstadt was convicted after evidence had been given by several security officers.'

Ah.

Keeping very cool and level-headed, Grau tried to analyse that. 'Several security officers.' Maybe that wasn't so unusual. After all, the men who had arrested him were bound to give evidence. And then somebody must have questioned him. So that would make two or three, at least.

Don't worry about it, Grau said to himself. The sloppy way British journalists do things, 'security officers' could just be policemen anyway.

But then, he kept worrying about the two-day trial bit. How could a spy put up a two-day defence? It's not like a murder case. He can't say, I didn't do it.

Or could he? Could he say, for example, I am not a Nazi, I was intending to work with British Intelligence, only I got caught before I could come over to you? Could he have tried to buy his life with cooperation?

Grau put the papers in the rubbish bin.

It was no use becoming neurotic. The case had nothing to do with him. A colleague had fallen, that was all. His own operation had nothing to do with it.

All the same, decided Grau, for the next few days he was going to be extra careful. The way things were moving, it would be foolish to take chances.

26

They came for Clare in the middle of the night. The door was kicked open, a blinding light glared into her eyes, and a voice snapped:

'Get up.'

She didn't even have a chance to look at the time.

'What is it?' she managed to say.

'You're coming with us,' said another voice. Dimly she was aware that there were two of them, at least two, perhaps three.

She tried to clear her head.

'Who are you?'

'Get dressed,' said one of the voices, roughly.

'I can't see,' she said.

The electric light was switched on, and now she saw there were three men. One had a roll-neck sweater and wore dark glasses. The other two were in raincoats.

'What do you want?' she asked, screwing up her eyes in the sudden light.

'Come on, come on,' said dark glasses impatiently.

One of the others tossed her underwear on the bed.

'Hurry up,' he said.

'Is this a joke?' said Clare.

'You're under arrest,' said dark glasses.

Now her head was clearing, and she understood. This was the special test.

'One day you may get the Gestapo treatment,' Maguire had warned her, early on. 'You'll get interrogated, just like the real thing. They'll try to make you crack. They'll use any method they think may break you. It can happen at any moment. They want to see how you will stand up to it.'

My name is Justine Renoir. That is what she must say. I come from the village of Dhuizon in the Sologne. My parents are dead. I am in Paris looking for work. That was the cover identity she must remember.

'Up,' snarled one of the men in a raincoat.

'I'll get dressed as soon as you leave the room,' said Clare.

'You get dressed now,' said dark glasses, who seemed to be in charge.

'We've seen tits before,' said one of the others, and they all laughed.

She slipped on her bra, and the rest of her underwear while they all watched. The back of her neck prickled.

Dark glasses threw a raincoat at her.

'Put this over it,' he said.

'I want to put on some clothes,' she protested.

'You've got enough on,' said one of them.

'Let's go,' snapped dark glasses.

They marched her out of the room, and down the corridor, and it struck her that nobody seemed to have heard the noise.

Outside the building a car with no lights was parked, and she was flung into the back. One of the raincoats got in beside her, and she was roughly blindfolded.

'You can't just break into my quarters—' began Clare.

'Shut up,' said the man, and slapped her. Hard.

So this is what they meant by the real thing.

It was a short, bumpy drive, and she had no idea where they took her. Suddenly the car stopped, she was hustled out, nearly fell over some steps, evidently an entrance to some other building, then down, down into what appeared to be a basement. She heard a door being unlocked, and was half-pushed, half-dragged into a room.

Then she was dumped on a kitchen chair. Somebody ripped off her blindfold, and she saw she was in a bare room – bare except for a table and the chair on which she sat. A naked electric bulb hung from the ceiling.

The three men stood in front of her. She vaguely thought there was somebody behind her too, but she wasn't sure. She tried to turn her head, and was hit.

'You move when we tell you,' said dark glasses pleasantly.

'Now, Miss,' said one of the raincoats. 'Let's have the truth.'

'Your name?' said one of the others.

'My name is Justine Renoir,' she said.

'Your real name,' said dark glasses.

'I've told you. Justine—'

'All right,' he cut her short. 'We have plenty of time. Date of birth?'

'Second July 1922.'

'Place of birth?'

'Rouen. But I've lived most of my life in Dhuizon. You know Dhuizon? In the Sologne.'

They stared at her, silently. Then dark glasses sighed.

'I think you've got this all wrong, Miss Gilbert,' he said patiently. 'We're not asking you for your cover story. We want to know about you.'

Clare licked her lips. She didn't understand this. She had a field name, which the other side should never know. And she had her cover name. Her real name wasn't part of the exercise.

'We're security people, Miss Gilbert,' said dark glasses. 'We want to know some things urgently. We're not interested in the games you play here.'

'I don't know what you're talking about,' she said. She was sure there was somebody behind her.

'Let's start all over again,' said one of the men in the raincoat. 'You got off the train in London, and you made a phone call. Who to?'

This is crazy, thought Clare. The thing has to be played according to the rules. They're mixing up the real thing with the fiction.

'Who did you phone?' repeated dark glasses.

'You mean, when I went on leave?'

Dark glasses nodded.

'That's right,' he said agreeably. 'Now you know what we're talking about.'

'I don't see what this has to do with the test,' she said.

'What test?' asked one of the men.

'The interrogation. The Gestapo routine.'

'I think you're confused, Miss Gilbert,' said dark glasses

kindly. 'Just answer what we want to know. Who did you call?'

All right, she thought. I'll do it your way. But I wished the briefing had given a hint about this.

'My father,' she said.

'Who is . . .?'

'He works at the Ministry of Economic Warfare. His office is in Berkeley Square.'

Dark glasses nodded again.

'Then you met a man at the Savoy. That was your father?'

'Yes,' she said, 'but . . .'

'But what, Miss Gilbert?'

She shook her head.

'Did you meet anyone else at the Savoy?'

'No,' said Clare.

Dark glasses sighed.

'I wish you'd tell us the truth,' he said reproachfully. 'You made contact with somebody else.'

'No,' said Clare.

One of the raincoated men approached her chair, his fist clenched.

'You must be anxious to hide something,' said dark glasses. 'Otherwise you wouldn't be lying. You spoke to somebody else.'

She really had forgotten. Then it came to her.

'Oh, I said hello to – Martin.'

'Martin?'

'He's an officer here. At least, at the base, that's where I met him. He's – he's . . .'

'Yes, Miss Gilbert?'

'My father thinks – he might be something to do with security . . .'

'Why?'

'He's seen him somewhere. At the Ministry.'

They stared at her, in that silent, unfriendly way.

Dark glasses pulled out some cigarettes, offered Clare one. She shook her head. He lit one for himself.

'You take over, Garton,' he said.

Garton, one of the raincoated men, smiled coldly.

'After you left your father, where did you go?'

'I met a friend.'

'Where?'

'A service club.'

'Be precise, Miss Gilbert. You went to the Grosvenor House, the US officers club, and you kept an assignation there with Captain Anthony R. Waymaster, of the 96th Bomb Gp, 8th Air Force.'

'I had a date, not an assignation.'

Garton stared at her.

'You seemed anxious to avoid company. You left straight away and went to the Dolphin, in Shepherd's Market. But you didn't stay there very long.'

Clare was silent.

'Then you did a curious thing. You and Capt Waymaster went to a – er – rather cheap establishment in Paddington. Why there?'

'You tell me,' said Clare, furious. 'You know it all.'

'American soldiers are not badly paid,' said Garton.

The other two laughed.

'They get more than I do,' said dark glasses.

'You booked into the Phoenix commercial hotel, bed and breakfast with double room fifteen bob,' said Garton. 'And you stayed there under false names. Why?'

'I didn't give any name,' said Clare.

'Captain and Mrs Brown,' said Garton. 'Really.'

Clare clenched her hands.

'What is the point of all this?' she snapped.

'The point is,' said dark glasses, 'that we are very curious about you.'

'Why?'

'My name is Justine Renoir. I am twenty-two. My parents are dead. I am looking for a job in Paris. I come from Dhuizon ...'

She might as well have been talking to a wall.

'Stand up,' snapped Garton.

She rose.

'Take that raincoat off.'

Clare hesitated.

'Take it off,' said Garton, and his tone said if you don't, we'll do it for you.

She let it slip off, and stood in front of them half naked, dressed only in her skimpy underwear. She shivered.

Then, from behind her, appeared the person whose presence she had felt all along. He was tall, and had a grey moustache. She had never seen him before, but the others almost imperceptibly stiffened to attention.

'That'll be all,' he said.

He looked at her thoughtfully.

'Put that coat on, Miss Gilbert,' he said. But there was no sympathy in his voice.

He turned to the man in dark glasses 'Take her back,' he ordered.

'Come along,' said dark glasses.

'You should have done better than this, Miss Gilbert,' said the man with the moustache. 'At this rate, you're liable to give the whole show away before they've even started on you.'

All the way back in the car, Clare was sobbing. But she did not know if it was rage, or fear.

27

Grau had fixed a bell on the door of the bookshop, so that even if he was in the back room he could hear as soon as somebody entered.

Not that anybody was likely to sneak in and steal a book. It was simply part of his system to ensure that he was never taken by surprise. He hated the idea of people prowling around. He didn't mind them browsing, if he was sitting in a corner, but he wanted to know that they were there.

Grau took the musty, second-hand bookshop quite seriously, and he offered good value for anyone who bothered to look around. He had specialities, like Edgar Wallaces, rows and rows of them, some selling at threepence, and Henties. He was proud of having a special line in Henties. What was more eminently respectable than selling the kind of book that even Victorians thought suitable for a Sunday school prize. True, they were really schoolboy literature, but how could he go wrong with titles like *True to the Old Flag*?

Sometimes Grau bought books off people who brought a pile into the shop. He didn't encourage this, but he felt a second-hand bookseller could hardly shut his door to that kind of deal.

Once a bearded man had come in and offered him two English translations of *Mein Kampf*.

'What do you want for these?' Grau asked him, peering at the stranger.

'Half a crown for the lot,' said the man.

'I don't like selling this kind of thing,' said Grau.

'Hitler's worth reading,' said the man, and instinctively Grau felt he ought to be wary.

But the man was quite sincere.

'How can you know what you're fighting if you don't know what's it all about,' he said. 'It's like talking about Communism without having read Marx.'

'I know what it's about,' said Grau. He offered the man two shillings, and he took it. Grau immediately locked the books in a cupboard. The last thing he wanted was to have somebody say that he sold *Mein Kampf*.

The bell rang, and Grau, who had his back to the shop, stacking some books, called out, 'Be with you in a minute.'

'No hurry,' said a voice. 'All the time in the world, Mr Harris.'

Grau tensed. People who come into a seedy little second-hand bookshop off Willesden Green don't usually know the name of the owner.

And he knew that voice.

He turned, and there he was, in RAF uniform, light-blond eyelashes, pimples, and all.

The landlady's son.

'This is a surprise,' said Grau, and he meant it.

'Just thought I'd have a look at your place,' said young Croxley.

'Oh yes?'

'Nothing much else to do.'

Damn, thought Grau.

'You're very welcome,' he said, and his tone sounded humbug even to himself. 'Make yourself at home.'

'Ta,' said Jimmy.

He walked over to one of the shelves and peered.

'Pretty heavy stuff you got here,' he said.

'Not really. All kinds.'

Croxley took out a book.

'I mean, look at this. *The Influence of Geography on History*. Blimey. That isn't going to set the Naafi alight.'

'Something here for every taste,' said Grau.

All the time, his mind was trying to sort it all out. How the hell did Croxley know where his shop was? And why did he bother to come?

He cursed that he couldn't remember whether he had in fact told his landlady the address. If he had, he could rest easy. But if he had never mentioned it . . .

It was a bad slip-up. He should always be able to remember instantly what he had told people.

'How do you manage to make a living out of all this?' asked Jimmy. Only the word junk was left out.

'I get by,' said Grau.

'Can't see 'em queueing to buy,' said the unbearable young man.

'I thought you only had twenty-four hours' leave,' said Grau.

'That's right.'

'Well, aren't you due back soon?'

'I'm going back at lunchtime.'

'Have a good journey,' said Grau.

Was he checking up on him? Grau felt increasingly uneasy. Why bother to find the shop? What was he after?

'Would you like to read something on the train?' he asked.

Jimmy sniffed.

'Don't imagine you have my kind of stuff. I don't go in much for a heavy read.'

'Perhaps a thriller?'

Jimmy leered. 'If you've got something spicy . . .'

Grau smiled. The man was a moron. Why should he get worried about him?

'Maybe something with crumpet,' said Jimmy hopefully. 'You know, a bit of what . . .'

'For what good, said Alice, is a book without crumpet or a bit of what . . .' misquoted Grau, but it was beyond Jimmy.

'Eh?'

'Nothing,' said Grau. He took down a couple of paperbacks. 'Here, try these.'

They came from the pile marked 'Everything Here Twopence'.

'Any good,' said young Croxley doubtfully.

'Try them,' said Grau. 'Bound to have a bit of – crumpet,' he added encouragingly.

Jimmy took the books. He shifted his feet.

'I'd like to ask you something, Mr Harris,' he said.

'Yes?'

'What are your plans?'

'What plans?' asked Grau, cautiously.

'Do you plan to stay at our place? I mean, Mother is entitled to know.'

'I like it very much where I am,' said Grau, wondering what he was getting at.

'She's on her own, and I just want to be sure . . .' said Jimmy.

'Sure about what?'

He shuffled again.

'That she'll be all right . . .'

Grau decided he had had enough.

'Has she asked you to say this? Is she asking?'

'Well, no,' said Jimmy uneasily.

'Well, I suggest you leave all that to her,' said Grau.

Young Croxley had come to a complete halt. Grau knew he didn't have the guts to continue.

He was right.

'Well, I'd better get going,' said Jimmy. 'Mustn't be back late . . .'

'Wouldn't do to be a deserter now, would it?' said Grau, with charm.

Jimmy scowled.

'I'll see you.'

He went to the door, then remembered the two books he was clutching.

'Ta for these,' he said grudgingly.

'Pleasure,' said Grau. 'See you on your next leave.'

The bell rang, and Jimmy was gone.

Bloody fool, thought Grau. But nevertheless, he felt a sense of relief that Croxley was no longer in the shop.

And yet he could not resist a smile at the thought that Jimmy had stood just a few feet from the two floorboards in the back room.

The floorboards which concealed the short-wave radio which was the direct link between Grau and Germany.

28

When Maguire asked to see Clare, she had no idea what was coming. He tended to keep things informal, and often mentioned something important when they met casually, in the corridor, or in the cafeteria, as if it were a sheer accident.

So she was surprised at being asked to go to the room with the french windows where he did his paperwork.

'Sit down,' said Maguire.

Clare tried hard to keep her eyes away from the two stumps on his right hand that had once been fingers.

'I'm sorry about the other night,' she said.

'The other night?'

He seemed genuinely puzzled.

'The interrogation, sir. I know I made a mess of it . . .'

'Oh that. It happens.'

She had been worrying about it ever since, and now she wanted to get her own side of it in first.

'It wasn't what I'd been briefed to expect,' said Clare.

'You don't have to explain.'

'I think it's important,' said Clare. 'I'd been expecting an interrogation. But I thought they'd try to trip up my cover story . . . not real things.'

'You mean fact and fiction got mixed up?'

'It was horrid. They must have been watching me every minute in London.'

'They work their own way,' said Maguire. 'Never mind.'

He was surprisingly kind.

'I only hope it hasn't affected my chances,' said Clare.

'I wouldn't worry about it.'

The pause that came seemed a long one. If that isn't what he wants to talk about, why did he send for me? wondered Clare.

'We've had some rather sad news,' said Maguire suddenly.

'What do you mean?'

'A friend of yours,' said Maguire.

'I don't understand . . .'

'Captain Waymaster,' said Maguire.

Tony? What was he talking about.

'I'm afraid that Captain Waymaster has been killed.'

She was numb. She didn't understand any of it.

'I'm sorry, Clare,' said Maguire, gently.

'But how – what's happened?'

'His plane has been lost. A B-24, I think.'

He looked at her with dispassionate interest.

Clare shook her head.

'Why me? Why are you telling me? I'm not his next of kin . . .'

'He must have given instructions to tell you – if it happened.'

'He didn't even know I'm here,' said Clare.

She knew she should be saying other things. She should cry, or rush from the room, or bite her lip bravely and ask for a cup of tea.

'He must have been very fond of you,' said Maguire.

'But how did they get hold of – here?'

'Through the War Office,' said Maguire.

Clare sat very tense.

Then, quietly: 'Where did it happen?'

'They haven't said,' murmured Maguire. He obviously wanted to finish this.

'Perhaps he's a prisoner?'

'I wouldn't raise any false hopes,' said Maguire.

'They don't suggest that he's merely – missing. I think they know the plane was, well, that it's been lost in action.'

'Thank you for telling me,' she said.

'Something I'd rather not,' said Maguire. 'Do you want a few hours on your own?'

'No,' said Clare. She looked at Maguire. 'We were – just friends. Nothing serious. I didn't even realize . . .'

'That he wanted you to know straight away?'

'I had no idea.'

Maguire went with her to the door.

'Had you known him long?' he asked.

'Not long,' she said vaguely.

'I'm sorry,' he said again.

As she left, he became official again.

'Don't forget to get a few hours' sleep today,' he said. 'You know what lies ahead tonight.'

'I know,' said Clare.

29

'The woman saboteur is one of the most dangerous weapons in our arsenal,' said the man from MIR, the research think tank. He looked round the ten people he was lecturing and gave a slight nod to the three women.

'Let me quote somebody like Veronique,' he continued. 'Of course, her name is not Veronique at all.'

They tittered appreciatively, like pupils in any classroom when the teacher makes a feeble joke.

'At latest count, Veronique has been responsible for the liquidation of a German staff officer, the destruction of some two hundred high-tension electricity pylons, the gutting of a German barracks, the blowing up of several locomotive sheds, and at least fifteen derailments of troop trains moving east to Germany and the Russian front. We estimate that in her various operations, she has been successful in killing and wounding perhaps four to five hundred German officers and men.

'And she's really just a slip of a girl, almost as pretty as you.'

All eyes turned on Clare, sitting next to Margit, the Polish girl.

'And you,' added the MIR man diplomatically, smiling at Margit.

He droned on, but Clare was staring past him at the map of France on the wall. The news about Tony had been more of a shock than she realized. She had slipped into the lecture after seeing Maguire, and now she only just began to be aware of what he had said. It was like a wound that had begun to throb.

'No housewife has ever been able to rely as much on her grocer as you will be able to on us to keep you supplied,' said the MIR man reassuringly. 'The usual standard drop will be of twelve containers to build up the resources of your circuits. You can reckon that the average drop should yield 6 Bren guns, 36 rifles, 27 Stens, five pistols, 40 grenades and detonators, explosives, fuses, field dressings, and maybe 20,000 rounds of assorted ammunition. Of course, the goodies can be varied. Veronique, for example, just adores the American ·30 carbines, so we send her those instead of the rifles.'

Clare was thinking about later that night. This was something she actually looked forward to. It meant action, movement. She could not really face another batch of lectures, people drawing complicated diagrams on blackboards, explaining about the temperament of explosives, cautioning, warning, alerting, briefing; she wanted to do something.

Going to her quarters, she bumped into Sadler.

'Get some shut-eye,' he said.

'That's where I'm off to,' said Clare.

'Good. You'll need your wits about you.'

'Are you cooking up something special?'

Sadler grinned.

'Wouldn't tell you if I knew, would I?'

'I hope I do it all by the book,' said Clare.

'You'll be fine,' he said. 'Now forget all about it.'

But she lay on her bed, and could not sleep, and when they called her at 2 AM she was much too eager to go.

30

The test was simple. She had to get through the wood to a gamekeeper's lodge without being caught.

She knew that all the time she would be hunted by the other side. They would lie in wait, hide behind bushes, lurk in the branches of trees, lie concealed in the dark, and their one job was to catch her.

The hunters and the hunted were all classmates, and both were eager to show how much they had learnt. They also knew that this game, played on a fine, moonlit night in an English wood, could be life or death for them perhaps in only a few weeks.

For there could well come the time, over on the other side, when they might have to get through a German-infested area, with a vital message, and if they were caught it could mean the firing squad not just for them but their whole circuit.

Or, paradoxically, they might have to be the hunters for real, to catch the traitor or the German counter-agent who had infiltrated their lair, and was now fleeing, with their secrets in his head.

So it was a training exercise with a purpose. A grim, bloody purpose.

The important thing was, as she was told in the briefing by the light of an oil lamp, not to be spotted. Once you were seen, basically you had lost.

'Of course you might still get away, but you've messed it up,' said Sadler. 'Ideally, you want to turn yourself into a ghost. Get invisible.'

Ghostlike Clare looked too, her face blacked. She wore a battledress, and leather gloves.

'When you're told to start, set off quickly. Don't worry about anybody else. Just get through. Good luck.'

The way though the wood was reasonably easy to follow, and Clare had studied a map of the area, and knew the lay of the land, and where the lodge stood.

What she didn't know was how many were pursuing her. Whether they had a head start, or were trying to catch up. Whether they already lay in place, waiting to ambush her, or she would hear them coming in pursuit.

She started out filled with excitement. She knew she was going to get through. She didn't know how many might be after her, two, three, or twenty, but she'd give them the slip, and elude them, and show them all.

She knew that she mustn't make much noise, and that the breaking of a twig could sound as loud as gunshot, and home them in on her.

So she started at a fast trot, but slow enough to see where she stepped, and to be able to look for any tell-tale trace of a hunter lying in wait, ready to pounce on her.

Deeper and deeper she went into the wood. She came into the

clearing where the two huge oaks grew, and for a moment she came to a complete halt, listening. But there was no suspect sound, no hint of anyone on her trail.

Clare was looking for the Plague Stone, a huge boulder. Legend had it that at the time of the Black Death food was left here for the inhabitants of a long since vanished village. The plague had taken hold of the village, and the people were not allowed out into the surrounding countryside. But some charitable souls would put food on the Plague rock, and leave it there for the dying villagers to collect.

That Plague Stone was a navigational beacon for Clare, and when she found it she knew that she was near the lodge.

She had been running fast, and now she decided to rest for a moment or two. She was surprised that she had heard or seen nothing. The hounds that were supposed to catch her hare seemed singularly unsuccessful. She couldn't understand why they had not picked up her trail. After all, she had taken a more or less direct route through the wood.

Even as she leant against the tree, she did see a movement a few yards away. She froze. Then she saw him. One of the agents was searching for her, looking cautiously around him as he moved forward.

Clare watched fascinated as he suddenly, for some reason, made up his mind that she might be somewhere in the wood to his right, and disappeared in the undergrowth in that direction. If only he knew how near he had come.

Way in the distance she could hear a train. Sound carried far in the night. And, in the darkness somewhere, came the throb of a plane, high, out of sight, the hum of its engines anonymous and detached.

She realized she was thirsty. Her mouth was dry. Enough hanging round here. On.

The lodge should be there any moment. She made her way through some thick undergrowth. Past another clump of trees. She was getting there. She was almost there.

'Sorry, Clare,' said a voice.

She spun round, and there stood a figure. In battledress. Like her. The face blacked out, a mask with two staring eyes. Like her.

No. She wasn't going to be caught. She could escape. She could make it.

She turned to rush on, but a hand grabbed her.

'Don't be silly, Clare,' said the voice. 'You're caught. It's over.'

She swung round, and reached for the figure that was clutching at her. She knew who it was. Another woman. Margit. The blonde Polish girl. The bitch, catching her just when she had made it.

'Keep off,' said Clare, through clenched teeth.

'It's the rules, Clare,' said the voice. 'Once you're caught, you give in . . .'

Clare hit her, and Margit reacted, just as she had been taught, and suddenly they were struggling, swaying to and fro.

Quite coolly, amid the panting and the hard breathing, Clare remembered Sadler.

'Disable them,' he kept saying.

The girls were not fighting like women, grabbing hair or using their nails as claws, they were wrestling like athletes, and then Clare managed to get Margit's right arm, and she turned it and twisted it, and Margit screamed.

'No—' she screamed. 'Don't!'

But Clare didn't let go, and Margit sank to her knees. She wanted to hurt her. She tightened her hold on Margit's arm. She kept pressing and pressing.

Clare saw the blonde hair tumbling. The bitch. Margit. Margaret. Blonde hair. She did not know suddenly what woman she was forcing to scream for mercy, all she knew was she was twisting and pressing—

'Have you gone crazy?' said a voice, and Sadler was pulling her off.

Margit had collapsed, and her right arm hung limply where Clare had broken it. Clare stood panting, her breasts heaving, her face flushed.

Sadler bent down and looked at Margit.

'My God,' he said.

He stood up.

'Are you mad or something?' he asked Clare.

'She – she tried to stop me,' she gasped.

'She was supposed to,' said Sadler. 'That was the point, wasn't it? To see if they can catch you. And you were supposed to give in. It's a bloody exercise, not the real thing, isn't it?'

'I'm sorry,' said Clare dully.

'We'll have to get help,' he said. 'You come with me.'

They walked to the lodge, leaving Margit lying like a broken doll.

'What did you do it for?' asked Sadler. 'She hadn't done anything to you.'

'I'm sorry,' repeated Clare.

But Sadler shivered a little. Because he knew she wasn't sorry at all.

31

'The girl would make a very good agent,' said the colonel.

'I agree, sir,' said Ince.

'More's the pity,' said the colonel. 'What about the Polish girl?'

'I'm afraid she won't be able to go operational for some time,' said Ince. 'The arm's badly fractured. You've seen the medical report.'

'And the Gilbert girl did that with her bare hands?'

'Yes, sir.'

'Sadler trains 'em well.'

'Sadler may have trained her a little too well,' said Ince.

'How's that?'

Ince indicated the folder in front of the colonel.

'Cleaver says it pretty bluntly. Miss Gilbert has been – affected by what she's been taught.'

'He says she's undergoing a period of emotional stress,' said the colonel.

'I've talked to Cleaver,' said Ince. 'The girl likes killing.'

The colonel stared at him.

'I'm afraid so, sir. We're lucky she didn't kill the Polish girl. This was a perfectly normal training exercise, and when she came up against it, the killer instinct came out.'

'Ince, I'm not sure that's a bad thing. Not for the kind of work we have in mind for her.'

Sometimes the colonel infuriated Ince.

'Yes, sir. But we don't want them to kill our own people. Cleaver feels this girl is not safe. Under operational conditions she might turn on anybody. On her own side.'

'She'll get over it,' said the colonel.

'Sir, she's emotionally disturbed. She should be invalided out.'

'Except she knows too much.'

'Exactly.'

The colonel stood up and looked out over Portman Square.

'I suppose if you take a perfectly nice pretty girl and you teach her how to kill, it could sometimes cause problems,' he said, more to himself.

'Well, it has,' said Ince.

The colonel faced him.

'So it's the Cooler?'

'What else can we do with her?'

Ince knew that the colonel had already made up his mind anyway.

'Very well,' said the colonel. 'Prepare the orders. Special training, and all that.'

'Very good, sir.'

'It's not very good at all, Ince,' said the colonel testily. 'We can't afford it.'

'Yes, sir,' said Ince.

'How's Loach settling in?'

'That's another problem,' said Ince.

But he did not elaborate.

Inside

32

The leather armchair near the fireplace was empty, and Loach sank into it with a copy of *The Times* he had picked up from the table.

He enjoyed the rich comfort of the oak-panelled library. It could be a club in St James's, and like a club member he had his favourite armchair, and resented it if somebody had got to it first.

And it was a club, after all.

Loach gave a cynical smile. Membership was very exclusive. Outsiders didn't qualify. Once elected, you couldn't resign. And as far as the outside world was concerned, you had vanished.

It took him a little time to fully realize this. When the staff car picked him up at the small railway station, and he found himself being driven through miles of Scottish countryside, he had no idea what to expect.

Inverloch, so they said, was something special. Secret training. Hush-hush stuff. Only for special people.

The car came to the end of a small country road, and two green-bereted Commandos suddenly appeared. They had side-arms, and they waved the car down.

The driver, who had not said three words to Loach, handed them some papers. One of the Commandos looked into the back of the car, saluted Loach, and then waved them on.

But they weren't there yet. More lonely lanes, and narrow, crooked country roads. Not a farmhouse, not a road sign, not a telegraph pole.

Finally, the long drive through the wood, and then the mansion, standing in beautiful grounds by the side of a loch. The car crunched to a halt on the gravel, and an RAF sergeant came out, and took Loach's bags out of the back. Loach was surprised to see the man in Air Force blue. Only later he found out that all kinds of uniforms staffed Inverloch . . .

Loach felt he seemed to be booking into a luxury country hotel, rather than reporting to a military establishment. In fact, it was even less formal than the hotel. There was no reception desk, no visitors' book to sign.

'I'll take you to your room, sir,' said the RAF sergeant. 'If you'll follow me.'

Up a beautiful ornate staircase, along a corridor with wood carved doors. They stopped at one of them, the sergeant opened it.

He took Loach's bags inside.

'I hope you'll be comfortable, sir,' he said, with the pride of a hotel manager who knows he is giving a guest good value.

'Yes, thank you,' said Loach, baffled.

They hadn't even asked him his name.

The room was wood-panelled, as so much in this house, the bed looked inviting. There were two comfortable armchairs, a bookcase, a small desk. And the windows looked out on the grounds, and the loch beyond.

A door led to a small bathroom.

'If there's anything you want, sir, just give us a buzz,' said the sergeant, indicating a bell-push in the wall.

The sergeant opened a wardrobe door.

'Shall I hang up your things, sir?'

Loach nodded.

'They're serving tea,' said the sergeant. 'If you'd like to go to the lounge ...'

'Tea!' said Loach.

'Downstairs, sir, and across the hall, on your left.'

'I'd like to report to the CO,' said Loach.

'Yes, sir,' said the sergeant and took no notice.

'Where is his office?' said Loach, sharply.

'He'll be getting in touch with you, sir, I'm sure,' said the sergeant, and finished hanging up Loach's clothes.

Loach gave up. What a unit.

After the sergeant left, Loach examined the room as he had been trained. It was an automatic ritual he followed whenever he stayed somewhere strange. It helped to keep him alert. So he looked at electric fittings, and light switches, and the wiring, and ornaments, and tapped walls gently, not expecting to find anything, but taking all the precautions that might save his life in a Bordeaux hotel or a Paris boarding-house.

Next the bookcase. He picked up one of the volumes. *Torquemada and the Spanish Inquisition.* Strange, thought Loach. Published 1924. Hardly the usual bedtime reading. And what was this? *A Record of Espionage and Double-Dealing, 1500–1815.* Next to it, de Sade's *Justine*, in French. And, apparently just for good measure, a couple of Ellery Queens.

Loach didn't expect the tap at the door when it came.

'Yes?' he called out.

The man who came in wore a tweed jacket and flannels, and smiled pleasantly.

'Captain Loach?'

'Yes,' said Loach again, cautiously.

'Colonel Shaw,' said the man.

'Sir?' said Loach.

'Oh, I forgot,' said the man. 'They probably didn't warn you how informal we are here. I'm the commanding officer.'

Discipline was not Loach's strong point, but even he hadn't come across anything like this.

'Welcome to Inverloch,' said the colonel.

'Thank you,' said Loach. 'I was just about to – to report to you.'

He became aware he was still clutching the de Sade book and hastily slipped it back into the bookcase.

'Please sit down, Colonel,' said Loach lamely.

Shaw dumped himself in one of the armchairs.

'We tend to do things our own way here,' he said pleasantly. 'I don't expect they gave you much of a briefing.'

Loach pulled out the sealed letter.

'Major Ince asked me to give you this,' he said.

'Thank you,' said Shaw, and put it in his pocket without the slightest interest. 'How is everything?'

'Pretty frantic,' said Loach. He was conscious of Shaw studying him. To hell with it. He might as well be honest. 'We've had a few problems,' he said.

'Who hasn't?' said Shaw.

'I don't quite know what I'm doing here, actually,' said Loach. 'My orders were cancelled at the last moment.'

'Didn't they tell you anything?' asked Shaw.

'Not really.'

'Typical,' said Shaw, sympathetically.

But no more than that.

Loach tried again.

'Major Ince said something about special training.'

Shaw nodded.

'I must say I find that strange,' said Loach. 'I've been over there several times. I've learnt more in the field than anybody can teach me in school. I don't understand what special training I need.'

'Things are changing,' said Shaw vaguely. 'We really have a job to keep one step ahead.'

'How long will the course take?'

'Oh, it depends,' said Shaw. 'It's very specialized, you see.'

'But you understand my point of view. I want to get going again. Things are building up over there. That's where I can be useful.'

'Of course.'

'I don't know how much you know about F Section, Colonel...'

'Just a little,' said Shaw. 'People like Viner. And Etienne. You get to know them.'

The colonel excused himself and after he had left Loach was no better informed about Inverloch than before.

But what Loach could not forget was the mention of Viner and Etienne. They had worked with Loach. But they had never talked about Colonel Shaw.

And they were both dead.

33

Everybody in the place wore civilian clothes, except some of the conducting officers, and the NCOs from the three services.

Loach met the adjutant, and was given a timetable of lectures and study groups they wanted him to attend. And, for the first time, he began to be conscious that the men and women who were undergoing the same training seemed to know no more what it was all about than he did.

The usual security rule about not asking personal questions was strictly enforced.

There was a girl Loach rather liked.

'How long have you been here?' he asked her.

'I've only just come,' she said.

'Special training?'

She nodded.

'I'm Captain Loach. James Loach.'

'My name's Clare.'

'Clare . . .?' He paused halfway.

'Let's leave it at that,' she said.

He tried to get near her whenever he could. If he saw her ahead of him in the grounds, he'd catch her up and start chatting. She was pretty, and her figure was tempting, only she seemed wary. Of him and everyone else.

Within the mansion and the vast grounds, they were all at complete liberty. But that was where it stopped.

'Because of the sensitive nature of our work, we have a special security problem,' said the bald man who called Loach into his office to give him the lecture they all received. 'That means complete isolation. Nobody must know where this place is, or what we do here. No phone calls can be made. No letters can be received or sent directly.'

Loach had noticed the lack of telephones. He had not seen one since he arrived, except in the bald man's office, and on the adjutant's desk.

'When do we get some leave?' asked Loach. 'I'd like to go to London for a few days some time.'

'I'm sorry,' said the bald man. 'No leave while you're here.'

'How about an evening out . . .'

The bald man shook his head.

'Actually, there's no point to it,' he said, with a chuckle. 'There's nowhere to go . . .'

'There must be a pub somewhere . . .'

'I'm sorry,' said the bald man again.

'You make this sound like a prison,' said Loach.

'Jerry would give his right arm to know what's going on here,' said the bald man.

'Really?' said Loach, and he sounded sceptical.

'You'll have to take my word for that,' said the bald man. 'In any case, Captain Loach, it won't be for long. And every kind of recreational facility is provided here. You won't find time hanging heavily.'

He chuckled again merrily.

The bald man was right too. They could fish in the loch. The library was beautifully stocked. Every daily paper and most magazines were available. There was a music room, and well-run record recitals every Thursday. Billiards and table tennis were laid on. There was a gym, and miles of countryside to go walking.

And, in a curious way, although security was rigidly enforced, personal relationships were almost encouraged. Loach soon became aware that some of the men and women did not just meet over a meal, or in the lounge. Sometimes there were footsteps in the corridors at night, and the sound of doors being gently opened or shut.

Loach started feeling the need for a woman. And the woman he wanted was Clare. She was still aloof, charming, friendly, yes, but not a hint of any readiness for some emotional involvement. Once Lacch could break through that ice barrier, he knew there would be no problem. He could take her to his room, and spend the night with her, and if she was still in the bed when the orderly came in the morning, nobody would raise an eyebrow. The orderly would probably merely say, 'Two teas this morning, sir?'

If it ever got that far...

He saw her coming down the ornate staircase, and called out.

'Clare.'

'Yes?'

'Listen, do you play chess?'

That was the last thing she had expected.

'Why, yes,' she said. The smile was quite genuine too.

'Why don't we have a game, tonight, after dinner?'

She nodded. 'Why not?'

Well done, Loach, he said to himself.

'In the library,' he said.

He hadn't been aware that Colonel Shaw had heard it all.

'Nice work, Loach,' said the colonel.

It left Loach with the uneasy feeling that he had done exactly what the colonel wanted him to do.

34

Outside it was pouring, and Grau sat in the pub in Edgware Road, slowly getting drunk. He knew what he was doing, and that his inbuilt caution would not let it go too far. He knew he mustn't end up in the street waving his arms and shouting, or slumped in a doorway. That meant trouble.

But tonight he needed to get high. The constant routine, the eternal looking over his shoulder, the awareness of what he was supposed to be and who he really was had got him to the point where he needed to do something he shouldn't.

Perhaps, if he had a woman he could trust, this would be the fatal night when he muttered something, in her arms, that could lead him to the gallows.

Grau trusted no one. And in a moment like this, when his

self-discipline had reached cracking point, he knew the only safe thing was to be alone with himself.

He couldn't face going back to his room. If that idiot landlady started yapping, he might say the words that could cause disaster. Or, at least, force him to find somewhere else to live, and that would be both awkward and risky.

So Grau went into the pub, and ordered a Scotch and to his surprise they had some whisky, and he ordered another one, and now the warmth was seeping through him and his head felt just a little light.

But he was still a camera, taking in the people in the saloon bar, the GIs from the Victory Club across the road, the dull civilians, the blowsy girls, the damp raincoats, and rivulets of water on the floor from the umbrellas.

And his camera eye focused on the girl sitting at the table next to his. She was quite alone, and she had been drinking steadily, and her lipstick was smudged.

With a shock, Grau realized that she was looking straight at him. There was one terrible thing about the girl. An ugly, evil scar ran jaggedly across her face, turning her mouth into a sneer and marring her cheek.

If she had not had that scar, she would have been beautiful. With it, her face was a macabre cartoon. She was hideous.

Grau was fascinated by her. He looked at the wedding ring on her finger and wondered what man would have married a woman with such a fearful disfigurement. Of course, she might be very good in bed, and anyway in the dark . . .

She was still looking at him, and Grau was sufficiently drunk to be reckless. He called over the waiter, ordered himself another Scotch, and then leant over:

'Another one?' he asked.

'Gin,' she said.

Grau, without being invited, moved to her table. There was no reaction from her.

'Filthy night,' said Grau.

'Yes.'

The drinks came, and Grau paid.

She drank her gin without a word, just giving him a slight nod.

'They must have good connections here,' said Grau.

She looked at him without interest.

'I mean . . . they don't seem to run out . . .'

He was stammering. Perhaps it was the warmth, or the whisky, or her eyes boring into him.

'One more?' said Grau.

'One more,' she said.

When she spoke, that awful scar twisted with the movement of her mouth and made her face even more hideous.

Grau was pretty tight now. He had been drinking steadily for an hour.

'Do you want to sleep with me?' she asked.

Grau blinked. He couldn't have heard straight. All this noise in the pub.

She gave a bitter laugh.

'Don't worry. I don't blame you.'

Fleetingly, she raised one hand, and furtively touched the scarred face.

'It doesn't matter,' said Grau gently. He so wanted to be kind to her.

She swigged down more gin.

'Doesn't it?' she burped.

He shook his head.

'No,' she said. 'Forget it. Just forget it.'

Grau felt very hot.

'Take me home,' he said.

'Charity week, eh?'

'Don't be stupid,' he muttered.

'I'm no bloody charity,' she said, bitterly. 'You'll have to pay . . .'

'Of course,' said Grau.

'Give me two quid,' she said.

He gave her the money, puzzled. She stood up, a little too

carefully, and walked over to the bar. She said something to the barman, and she had a bottle under her arm when she came back to Grau.

'I'm round the corner,' she said.

They went into the wet, blacked-out street.

Grau had taken her arm. He felt her shiver.

35

When Grau saw her naked, there were other scars. One went right across her right breast, and the others criss-crossed her body.

Later, in bed, he lazily stroked her breast.

'How did it happen?'

'Battle scars,' she said, and her laugh was chilling.

'No, seriously.'

'I'm bloody serious,' she said. She giggled drunkenly.

They had drunk most of the bottle she had bought, and their speech was slurred and it took them a long time to formulate sentences.

'Your husband?'

'What husband?' said the girl.

Grau lay silent.

'What's your name?' he asked.

'Sylvia.'

'Who did it, Sylvia?'

She ignored him.

'That's all I ever was, a good fuck,' she said, but she might have been talking to herself. 'Now who wants to look at me . . .'

'I do,' said Grau.

'Maybe you're twisted, like him,' she said.

'Why did he do it?'

'He enjoyed it, dearie. That's what gave him his thrills. I wish I'd killed the bastard.'

'Did they get him?' asked Grau.

'Who?'

'The police.'

'You must be joking,' said Sylvia, and drank some more gin.

'Why,' asked Grau.

'Because they can tell the police to go to hell. Because they can tell me to go to hell.'

'Who's they?' said Grau, curious.

Sylvia turned to him, and her breasts brushed across his chest, and she kissed him.

'What do you care?' she said. 'It doesn't show in the dark.'

Afterwards, Grau said:

'You shouldn't let a maniac like that get away with it.'

'Forget it, darling,' said Sylvia. 'You're dealing with the cloak and dagger boys.'

Suddenly, Grau was very alert.

'Cloak and dagger?'

'Never mind,' said Sylvia. 'I'll never forget the bastard's name. I hope the Gestapo fries his guts in France.'

Grau said, very gently:

'What was his name?'

'Oh, it doesn't matter,' said Sylvia.

'Tell me,' said Grau. 'I want to know.'

'Loach,' said Sylvia. 'His name was Loach.'

36

Ince had been due to visit the monitoring people at Caversham for some time, but he never seemed to have a free moment to make the trip to Reading.

So when Simpson, the man from IB, phoned, and said he'd be at Bush House, and why didn't they meet there, Ince agreed at once. The way things were piling up, it might be a long time before he could find time to spend the day at the priory.

Ince knew his way round Bush House. He seldom wore uniform when he went there. It would seem out of place among the pipe-smoking journalists and university types in woollen cardigans who sat in the offices and shuffled along the corridors.

Very few of them had any idea of Ince's job. If he had to be introduced, it was as someone 'from the War Office'. And very few outsiders knew what some of them did. As far as the world was concerned, this was the BBC European service. And so it was, much of it.

The other bit nobody talked about.

Not many people, for instance, understood what the 'personal messages' were all about – the disjointed, meaningless sentences broadcast at the start of French language news bulletins.

'Marianne has eaten the apples.' 'The chicken will lay three eggs.' 'The oak tree stands tall.' 'Tonight the stars twinkle.'

Ince enjoyed composing family greetings which were complete nonsense, like 'Grandma will not bake the cake but sends you best wishes,' or 'Happy anniversary for Uncle Maurice and his beautiful Claudine'. What he liked was the thought of German code experts going out of their mind trying to unravel what was, after all, undecipherable.

It wasn't really Ince's job to devise the phrases, but, like Hitchcock in the background of a fleeting scene, he couldn't resist it.

Simpson knew his game, and tolerated it with some amusement.

They first started using the system, cautiously, back in '41, and now hundreds of messages went out each week, sometimes for fifteen solid minutes in one evening. They gave news, to those who knew the code, of agents landing in their zones, of supply drops, of hasty changes in plans, of couriers crossing borders, and operatives changing hideouts.

It was fool-proof.

At least . . .

'What's the problem then?' asked Simpson, who had been Reuter's man in Budapest at one time, as well as fulfilling another function which was not inscribed on his passport.

Ince shrugged.

'No problem. Just wondering ...'

For the messages were a key security safeguard for agents whose identity was questioned by their contacts.

'You don't believe I've come from London?' the agent was supposed to say. 'You don't think I'm in touch with them. All right. I'll prove it. Give me a phrase you want the BBC to broadcast, and I'll get them to send it over the air. Any phrase – birthday greetings for your wife, the first line of your favourite poem, anything ...'

And the contact would say: 'Prove it then. Have the BBC put out "Genevieve's onion soup is the best" next Thursday at 2100 ...'

Once that happened, the agent's bona-fides were guaranteed.

Of course, if the Abwehr could ever turn that fail-safe channel to its own advantage ...

'Any reason for thinking it's happened?' asked Simpson.

'Not really,' said Ince.

Simpson was too long at the game to be satisfied with that, but he didn't say anything.

Perhaps it dated back to the destruction of the Jester circuit. Twenty-four hours before Simone sent her radio warning that all was lost, that Marcel, Kleber, and Louis, three of the key members, were missing and the second radio had been lost, she had asked Bush House to transmit a security check.

'The rose has thorns' was the phrase, and dutifully it had been sent out on the midnight transmission.

Ince had done some checking at the time, but he could find no reason for the request. In fact, in his final briefing to Loach, he was going to ask him to find out what it was all about. Whose credentials were being challenged? Who had to be vouched for?

And then came Simone's frantic last message.

The end of Jester.

And the beginning of an uneasy doubt that kept bothering Ince at odd moments.

'I wish you'd tell us a bit more what's really going on,' said Simpson. 'Caversham's buzzing like a beehive, but we're really working blind. It would help, you know.'

Ince decided to do the good public relations bit.

'I know, I know, half the time we're in the same boat. But I can tell you one thing – we'd be sunk without you. You're doing fantastic work.'

'We're short of people, we haven't got enough equipment, some of them are working double shifts,' Simpson said ungratefully. 'Do you know, there aren't even enough typewriters...'

'Just like us,' said Ince.

'Like hell,' said Simpson. 'I'll take you to lunch.'

He nodded to an attractive blonde as they left the third-floor office.

'Who's she?' asked Ince, casually.

'Who? Margaret? Works with me in IB. Very able woman,' said Simpson.

'Is she at the priory?'

'Oh no, she's based here,' said Simpson. 'Edits the daily monitoring report on your stuff.'

'I'd like to meet her some time,' murmured Ince.

'Whenever you want.'

He gave Ince a swift look.

'You're a bit late, if that's what you're thinking. She's tied up with some bloke at the Economic Warfare Min. In Berkeley Square. They've got a big thing going.'

'That's not actually what I was after,' said Ince.

'I would be,' said Simpson as the lift came. 'But what's the use, stuck out in bloody Caversham.'

Toussaint stood in the lift as they entered, and held the green button so that the doors wouldn't slide closed on them.

'Thank you,' said Ince, and then recognized Toussaint. He nodded, and said to Simpson:

'I didn't know you had a visitor from Duke Street.'

'I pop in and out,' said Toussaint. 'It is the only way to keep up with one's friends.'

'Especially these days,' said Ince.

'I think we're getting our problems sorted out, my dear Major,' said Toussaint. 'If the politicians could leave us alone, there'd be no problem.'

They got out in the entrance hall, and Simpson said:

'I thought we'd go to Stewart's, across the road.'

It was a routine with him. He and Ince had never lunched anywhere else in the Aldwych.

But Toussaint was still hovering.

'Talking of old friends, Major,' he said. 'I wonder if you've seen anything of Captain Loach.'

'Should I?' said Ince, stiffly.

'He is in your section, and I wondered ... we are friends, so ...'

'Yes?'

Simpson was watching the two men intently. He didn't know what it was all about, but Ince seemed suddenly to harden and he wondered why.

'I am like the Kipling elephant,' said Toussaint. 'Always curious. It *is* an elephant, isn't it?'

'It is,' said Ince.

He started to go.

'I am so glad Captain Loach is all right,' said Toussaint. 'One always hears these rumours ...'

'What rumours do you hear?'

'There was some talk in Duke Street that the good captain has – has been compromised.'

'You know what they say about careless talk in wartime,' said Ince.

They left Toussaint in the lobby, showed their passes, and went out into the street.

In Stewart's, Ince spoke for the first time.

'What was Toussaint doing in Bush House?'

'He keeps in touch with our French service,' said Simpson. 'You know how neurotic this De Gaulle man is about anything we do with France. Toussaint sniffs out the land for him.'

But in Ince's head an alarm bell was ringing, and he could not shut it off.

37

Clare found herself sitting next to Loach at the morning session they were supposed to attend as part of – part of their what?

Special training? She found it hard to believe. The subject was 'methods of special interrogation', but it sounded more like a history lecture.

'Let us examine the "audencia de tormento", the process of torture used by the Spanish Inquisition,' said the man in front of them blandly. 'The three principal methods, used with great effect, were the rack, the hoist, and the water routine.'

He went into specific details while they listened, puzzled, confused.

'The game was always played according to the rules,' said the man. 'No man could be tortured more than cnce, unless new evidence had come to light. The Courts of Inquisition laid it down quite firmly that tortures could be continued on a victim, but must not be repeated...'

'What is the difference?' asked Loach.

'You're Loach, aren't you?' said the man, as if that answered the question.

'Yes,' said Loach. 'I don't understand the point you're making.'

'The Directorium of the Holy Office made it clear that it was legitimate to carry on torturing a man continuously, but that it would be barbaric and cruel to stop and then carry on as before,' said the man, like a university don explaining a simple formula to a difficult student.

'I don't understand the relevance of all this,' said Loach.

'Methods of interrogation are of great relevance to all of us, I should have thought,' said the man.

'Yes, the ones the Gestapo uses,' said Loach, 'not ancient history.'

'Shall we carry on?' said the man. And he did, going into loving descriptions of the bostezo, a short iron piece used to wedge open the victim's mouth during the water torture, and the garrucha, the hoist which suspended a man from a hook by his wrists while weights were tied to his feet.

'The whole thing's a waste of time,' said Loach, walking in the grounds with Clare afterwards. 'Haven't you noticed that, everything they tell us, everything they teach us doesn't matter?'

Clare had been wondering about it too.

The operational stuff they were being taught at Inverloch was elementary. The use of one-time pads. Wireless security. Identity cover. It went right back to the early days at Ferny Bank. She knew all this, and so did the collection of people she found herself with.

People like Loach. Like the other men and women who had also clearly been sent to Inverloch from their various sections and groups. Who watched each other cautiously, never really talked about themselves, and didn't seem quite sure what they were doing in the place.

'I'm beginning to wonder what we're doing here,' said Loach. 'Aren't you?'

'It's all useful . . .' said Clare, but she sounded doubtful.

'Useful my foot,' said Loach. 'It won't help me to face a grilling in the Hotel Lutetia to know what the Inquisition called the water torture.'

'You've been over, haven't you?'

'Yes,' said Loach. 'Haven't you?'

'Not yet.'

They sat down on a stone bench.

'Are you F Section?' asked Loach.

'Are you?'

Loach smiled.

'Well said.'

His eyes travelled along her slim legs, upwards, took in the curve of her breasts under the sweater, approved of what they saw.

'What's it like?' asked Clare. 'On the other side?'

'Don't you know France?' he said, surprised.

'Of course. But now. What's it like, doing the job there?'

'You mean, living a lie day and night and hoping they won't spot you?'

She nodded.

'I enjoy it,' said Loach. 'It's this place I can't stand.'

'We probably won't be here very long,' said Clare.

'You see that bloke over there, in the wind-cheater?' asked Loach. Clare followed his eyes, and saw a man slowly strolling near a hedge.

'I had a drink with him,' said Loach. 'He's F Section. He's been here eleven months.'

Clare frowned.

'Doing what?'

'He doesn't know,' said Loach, and smiled grimly.

'Eleven months,' repeated Clare. Her eyes met Loach's.

'What is this place?' she asked quietly.

'Something very nasty,' said Loach.

38

When it happened, it was quite unexpected.

It was Glover, the doodler, who suddenly raised it under the item on the agenda marked 'general security'. Until then, the coordination meeting had droned on as usual, and Ince had not said a word.

Then Glover held up his pencil, like a dealer making a discreet bid at an auction.

'Yes?' said the general.

'Question, Chairman,' said Glover.

'Well?'

'The ISRB operation at Inverloch,' said Glover. 'What exactly is going on there?'

Ince pressed the panic button.

'If I may, Chairman – I don't think that's really part of the agenda,' he said.

'I ask the question,' said Glover smoothly, 'because the minister has asked me.'

'I think Inverloch is a special training operation, isn't it?' said the general, who didn't really want to know. 'Under your organization, Major?'

He turned to Ince.

'Yes,' said Ince.

They waited expectantly. He said no more.

'Well?' said Glover.

'That's what it is, special training,' said Ince.

'What kind of special training?' said Glover.

Ince had always disliked the man. Now he was detestable.

'Chairman, I think it is a rule of procedure that one never discusses technical details . . .' began Ince.

'With respect,' said Glover, who had been a very successful barrister before he moved into Economic Warfare, 'no one is asking for technical details. But the purpose of this committee is security coordination, and I think we should coordinate. And so,' he added, without the least suggesting a threat in his tone, 'does the minister.'

The general cleared his throat.

'Yes. Well. Perhaps you could just answer Mr Glover's question in broadest terms, Major Ince?' he said.

All right, thought Ince. I'll play it by the rules, but I won't tell you a thing.

'Inverloch is a special training establishment for advanced operational needs,' he said. 'People are sent there on certain assignments.'

'It's very isolated, I believe?' said Glover.

'It's very secret, Mr Glover.'

'So is the London Cage, but it can still function in Kensington Palace Gardens,' said Glover.

'Well,' said the general hopefully. 'Does that answer your question?'

'Not quite, I'm afraid,' said Glover. He gave Ince a frosty look. 'Unfortunately, we have heard some rather disconcerting rumours about Inverloch.'

'Really,' said Ince.

'Rumours which suggest that those who go there don't – er – leave it.'

Christ, thought Ince.

'You don't suggest they shoot 'em?' said Wilcox genially, from the other end of the boardroom table. The Combined Ops man chortled.

'I only asked a question,' said Glover, mildly.

Ince felt angry.

'I'm surprised the minister can be bothered with such rumours,' he said, and realized at once that he had made a mistake.

'What the minister does is his own affair,' said Glover. 'There is a certain – ah – mystery about Inverloch which arouses curiosity and, perhaps, a degree of anxiety. What is this place?'

Who's put them on it, wondered Ince. Who's the bastard?

'It's really a lot of nonsense,' he said aloud. 'We use Inverloch to give highly sensitive training to people who are going on extremely delicate operations. The less known about it, the better. It's as simple as that.'

He could see Glover wasn't going to leave it there. What the devil did the man know?

But Ince was lucky, this time.

'Thank you, Major,' said the general with obvious relief. 'The tea seems to be late, gentlemen.'

39

The original instructions that authorized the establishment of the Cooler were typed on two pages, and only three copies, each of them numbered, existed.

Copy No 2 was held by the Section, and Ince kept it in his personal top secret safe.

He looked at it again now, as if to reassure himself that authority actually existed. The security coordination meeting had become uncomfortably curious. Of course, the cover story always worked, secret training of a specialized nature covered it beautifully. And yet...

Ince remembered the briefing about Inverloch.

'We try to make no mistake in selecting our agents,' the smooth man from Group B had said, 'but errors are bound to be made, gentlemen. Nobody is infallible. And what do we do then?'

As the secret instructions put it so crisply, only 'refractory' or 'unsuitable' agents would be placed in the Cooler.

'It's in their own interest, isn't it?' said the Group B man. 'They know too much. They know the techniques. The faces. We can't just let them go with that kind of knowledge in their heads, can we?'

The routine was clearly laid down:

1 Flawed agents would never be given the real reason. They would simply be told that they require additional special training.
2 They could never leave until the knowledge they had was valueless.
3 Their next of kin will be informed that the agents are on active service in the field. Salaries will be paid into banks as if they were operational.
4 The establishment would be known as a 'workshop', operated by ISRB.
5 No outside contact would be allowed.
6 The area around Inverloch would be declared a prohibited zone under the Defence Regulations to a radius of 10 miles, and no strangers would be allowed within that distance.

All perfectly simple.

The Group B man was reassuring about nothing ever going wrong.

And how could it? The civilian police would think it a hush-hush research establishment doing highly secret work – that was why the use of the name Inter Services Research Bureau was a stroke of genius.

And if something did leak out, who would get to know? A D-notice to all newspapers prohibited any mention of Inverloch. No letters would come from the place. No phone calls would be made from it.

'I really don't think we have anything to worry about,' said the Group B smoothie.

The whole thing was so secret the services, as such, were not told. Nor were the security agencies not directly concerned.

'Nothing to worry about ...'

Ince smiled wryly. The bastard should have been at the committee, trying to ward off the questions.

So far, their luck had held.

But one day ...

Ince got up and put copy No 2 back in the security safe.

When things blew up, he had better not be around.

40

Mrs Croxley was standing in the hall as soon as he opened the door.

'You should have let me know,' she said reproachfully.

'I'm sorry,' said Grau. 'I meant to call. I met an old friend ...'

'It's none of my business of course,' she sniffed, 'but one does get worried, you know.'

Grau had been out all night.

'I thought you must have had an accident,' said the Croxley. 'When I saw your bed hadn't been slept in.'

She stared at him accusingly, as if he had been unfaithful to her.

'This friend has a big flat, and it was so late, I stayed,' said Grau.

He hated himself for even attempting to go through the motions of explaining to the stupid cow, even if it was a lie.

'I thought you might have been run over in the blackout,' she burbled on. 'I nearly rang the police.'

Hell, he hadn't thought about that.

'You need never do that,' said Grau hastily. 'Nothing happens to me.'

'Well, how do I know?' she sniffed. Wasn't she just like her pimply son?

'We are on the phone, you know,' she went on.

'Yes, of course.'

He went to his room, and sat on the bed he hadn't occupied for twenty-four hours.

He indulged himself with the thought of calling in the idiot.

'Sit down, Mrs Croxley,' he'd tell her. 'I tell you why I wasn't all nicely tucked up. I met a tart, in a pub, in Edgware Road.

'She's good in bed. Half an hour with her is better than you've been with a man all your fifty years, you old bag.

'I'm seeing a lot of her. And what is it to you, anyway. I pay you the rent. So shut up.'

Yes it would be nice. To see her face, to watch her grow red with anger, and get all puffed up, and see her ample bosom heave with righteous indignation.

But of course, it mustn't be.

The routine must go on. He must really be very careful to appease this creature. The last thing he wanted was for her to ring the police, and start them becoming curious about her missing lodger.

The irony of it was of course that however much Mrs Croxley disapproved of her lodger's night-time dalliance, Colonel Reinecke would be delighted.

Sylvia was turning into the little jigsaw piece that often remained the hardest one to find.

Grau had to be careful now.

There were things about her that intrigued him.

Like the man who had scarred her for life. The man she called Loach.

Like the people who had brought her together with Loach. The people with whom Sylvia didn't want to have anything more to do.

Don't force it, Grau told himself. Take it gently, step by step.

He found it so intriguing that he had disregarded the transmission routine, and sent some unexpected messages on the radio set in the bookshop.

41

The request for a special security check on Toussaint was turned down.

'It's politics, I'm afraid,' the colonel said. 'We couldn't do it without letting Duke Street know, and in the present climate, that's asking for trouble.'

He saw Ince's reaction.

'I know,' he said. 'But you've got to live with it.'

'Every time something goes wrong, Toussaint knows about it,' said Ince. 'Therese is smashed, and he's onto it. Jester goes sour, and Toussaint has it. Loach goes into the Cooler, and Toussaint starts asking questions. He even said "compromised".'

He shrugged his shoulders.

'He might be in this office with us now, for all we know.'

'I think you're over-dramatizing,' said the colonel. 'He's just very well informed.'

'I wish we were,' said Ince. 'They can send in people without letting us know, they can set up operations on their own, they can demand special communications and no cipher for us, but if we so much as spit across the Channel without telling them, you'd think we have desecrated Napoleon's tomb ...'

'They're a sensitive lot,' said the colonel. 'Toussaint came over with De Gaulle, remember. And things like Dakar leave their scars ...'

'We've got our scars,' said Ince bitterly.

'Let's hope this new idea works,' said the colonel.

'New idea?'

'SPOC. The Special Projects Operations Centre. It's to amalgamate our network with Duke Street's lot. All one happy family.'

'And Toussaint?'

'Will be right there in the middle,' said the colonel. 'I told you, it's politics.'

'Yes, sir,' said Ince.

He started to go. He knew when it was hopeless.

'Oh, by the way,' said the colonel, 'there's just one little thing.'

It was a 'one little thing' which usually meant trouble, late nights, paperwork.

'Yes, sir,' said Ince, cautiously.

'It's probably nothing,' said the colonel, looking in the four or five files before him for the right piece of paper. 'Ah.'

He extracted it, and read it again.

'I'll be sending you over a copy of this,' he said. 'It's just a routine thing, but I know you'd like to be kept informed. Sylvia, isn't it?'

'What about her?'

'That business with Loach didn't do her any good,' said the colonel. 'Poor bitch.'

'She's been looked after,' said Ince.

'Perhaps not sufficiently,' said the colonel. 'She's told us to go to hell.'

'She was in hospital for quite a time and ...'

'And now she's getting rather independent.'

'She can't do us any harm,' said Ince, but there was the beginning of a worry growing in him.

'I hope not,' said the colonel. 'Anyway, I leave it to you.'

Great, thought Ince. Either way, I'm responsible.

'I think we ought to be rather careful about these comfort girls,' said the colonel, as a kind of parting shot.

'We are careful, sir.'

'Oh, I know. And I think it's a good idea. Laying on a touch of companionship as part of the furniture. Stops them picking up the wrong talent after they've been briefed. But it has risks, Ince.'

'Most things have, sir. But it's worked.'

'Indeed,' said the colonel. 'I just want you to make sure this – er – Sylvia isn't one of the risks.'

42

And the system had always worked well, Ince told himself. Maybe the Archbishop of Canterbury wouldn't approve, and it wasn't the kind of thing Vera Lynn sang about. But it solved one hell of a problem.

You couldn't put a man who was sitting in London, waiting to be dropped by parachute in Nazi-occupied Europe, in a hotel room by himself while he waited for fog to clear in Sussex.

Or a man whose mission had to be delayed for two or three days because a last-minute hitch had developed.

The civil servants would have liked it that way.

'We've got you a nice room at the Cumberland Hotel, bed and breakfast. Of course you can go out for meals, and during the day you can keep yourself busy, going for nice walks or listening to Myra Hess playing Chopin in the National Gallery.'

That's how they would have handled it.

The Section did it differently. It had little batchelor flats tucked away in central London, a mews in South Kensington, a little square in Bayswater, a block of flats in Seymour Place.

With everything provided. Drink. Books. Records. Somebody to clean the place. Food in the fridge. Everything. Except the most important.

When a Polish lieutenant, waiting to be flown to his assignment in Eastern Prussia, and spending seventy-two unexpected hours killing time, and drinking himself silly in his Section flat, had gone out, picked up a tart at the corner of Bayswater Road and Hyde Park Street, and brought her back to the flat, the idea was born.

There were those all for court-martialling the Pole, but Ince and a few others saw the solution to a great problem.

They began to recruit what, inside the organization, got to be known as Sherlock's Harem. Contrary to what the Abwehr later believed, Sherlock was not the cover name of a special operations officer. It was simply that Sherlock Mews, off Baker Street, housed the office which handled the organizational side of the 'companionship', as the colonel delicately put it.

The girls were utterly reliable. And, curiously, amazingly patriotic. All they knew was that, from time to time, they would get a phone call, asking them to go to a certain address.

And there they'd find a man, he might be English or French or American or Polish, usually charming and pleasant, sometimes taciturn or morose, who seemed to have an unlimited supply of alcohol, and a great urgency to get on with things. Some of the men were tense, obviously under strain, waiting for a phone call, a message, a summons. Others appeared relaxed, but always alert, and slightly remote.

The girls soon discovered that none of their clients liked to talk about tomorrow, or the next day, or next week. The future drew a blank. They were only interested in today, and their lovemaking was intense, and very unromantic.

Sherlock's Harem didn't mind. The girls were professionals. Indeed, their convictions for soliciting and their police records as street-walkers proved of great use in recruiting them. Not only as testimony of their professional status but also as an excellent security check. It was a safe bet that a girl who started as a Mayfair tart in 1939 was hardly placed there by German Intelligence for possible use in the bed of an SOE agent in 1944.

It wasn't a full-time job. The girls were paid a retainer, and then on daily or nightly rate as they were required.

They knew it was something to do with some mysterious set-up, but as far as they were concerned, it was some kind of hospitality arrangement. The office that called them liked to provide its gentlemen with home comforts.

When the girls went visiting, the men never paid. All that was done by the office. And the office was generous. The girl might only have stayed for two hours, but she'd get full night fee, always.

As part of the unwritten but clearly understood contract, the girls were given a medical check-up in a women's hospital near Lisson Grove once a month. And they were told not to talk to anyone, about anything.

The system took a great load off Ince's shoulders. No longer did he have to worry about safe houses being opened to pick-ups from the street, about people under top secret orders, and on the eve of critical missions, roaming round back streets, trying to find a tart and getting into hassles with drunk GIs and unsympathetic policemen, or disappearing in the bedsitters of whores where nobody could find them, and entire operations might be jeopardized.

'If the War Office ever finds out ...' the colonel had said fearfully, when Ince first put up the plan.

'They won't,' Ince promised.

'What about funds?'

'The words "special project" cover a multitude of sins,' said Ince.

'But can you trust the girls?'

'If a pro isn't discreet, she's out of business,' said Ince.

The girls were warned against emotional involvement with the men they met. And the men, when they came back from their missions, might sometimes ask about 'Helen' or 'Jenny' or 'that lovely redhead that came to the mews', and could they see them again, but, if need arose, there would be a lovely blonde or a delightful brunette instead, and that would console them.

And other men, of course, never asked after one of the girls again. Because they never came back.

Sylvia had been a very reliable recruit. And she was very professional. Ince felt pleased that she was free to soothe Loach. What had happened then was most unfortunate. But a special *ex-gratia* payment from Sherlock Mews should have compensated Sylvia a little . . .

Ince read the copy of the report the colonel had passed to him. It was worrying.

Sometimes a little knowledge could be a very dangerous thing indeed.

43

The chess game had become almost a nightly routine for Clare.

They never arranged it, it was just understood. After dinner, they'd find a corner in the library, and Loach would bring over the box with the chessmen and the board. They would sit under the oil painting of the Scottish laird whose family had been rulers of Inverloch for centuries.

Both played an unpredictable game. Loach knew little of classic gambits or famous end moves. He simply played as the mood took him, but always viciously, determined to master her, sometimes savagely exchanging knight for knight, bishop for bishop in a ruthless bloodletting which had little finesse but left Clare helpless, battered into submission.

Not that Clare was a bad player. But she liked the more traditional game, and never produced the curious flashes of originality that were in no chess book. Clare played like a lady, Loach never like a gentleman. Yet it was Clare who, if goaded enough, suddenly made a move which, sometimes, was the beginning of the end for Loach.

In one way, the night-time chess game was in itself a gambit.

Clare knew that Loach wanted to go to bed with her, and this little routine provided a good opening. For the routine of the place enabled them to sit in the library as long as they wanted, playing two, perhaps even three games. Then they would go off to their rooms, and the code of Inverloch made it easy for two of them to go to one room, if they so wished.

And that, clearly, was what Loach knew would happen one of these evenings. Perhaps nothing need be said. Perhaps they would just walk along the corridor, and look at each other, and he would open the door of his room, and she would come in . . .

'Are you married?' Clare asked him one evening.

'I was,' he said curtly.

But he wondered. Why did she want to know? Little Miss Puritan? Or was she thinking more about him than he had imagined? What a ridiculous question anyway, here, in this crazy place, virtual prisoners, a colony of people with a load of secrets who did not know what they were doing there, or how long they would stay, or even why they were there . . .

Yet she had asked it.

He moved his rook, and looked up, and found that she had not been watching the board, but was staring at him. Uneasily, he felt it wasn't the look of a woman looking at the man with whom she contemplated making love. Rather, it was the cold stare of an interrogator.

They had little contact with other inmates. That was the word, inmates. They were a mixed crowd. Army officers. Civilians. A FANY. Two Navy people. They seemed to have one thing in common – they had all suddenly been sent to Inverloch. They didn't discuss it. Nor what they had done before they came here. Now they all shared the same strange life. Pointless lectures. Classroom discussions. Training courses they had already completed once. And a meaningless daily life, which allowed them every kind of personal freedom. Except to be part of the outside.

Shaw, the commanding officer who always wore his sports

jacket and flannels, drifted among them, listening, nodding, approving, and never revealing anything. The adjutant stayed out of their way, and the bald man in charge of security was seldom seen.

Loach had been the one who, all along, was beginning to show signs of rebellion, needling the lecturers in the eternal classroom sessions, questioning the instructors about the purpose of the training.

But it was Clare who took the initiative.

'I'm going to tackle Shaw,' she said.

Loach, about to move a pawn, stayed his hand.

'The colonel?'

He sounded surprised.

'Colonel, commanding officer, whatever he is,' she said. 'I want to know what's going on. What they're trying to do. What we're doing here.'

Loach smiled mockingly.

'You really think he'll tell you?'

He moved his pawn. Clare must have expected the move, for she immediately shifted a bishop into an attack position. It wasn't at all what Loach expected.

'Tell me,' said Clare, 'when have you last had a letter here?'

'I don't get letters,' said Loach.

'When have you made a phone call, or received one? Where is there a phone?'

'The colonel has one. In his office.'

'Which one can't use. And who's had any leave from this place? Have you heard of anyone?'

Loach castled.

'Don't you find it very pleasant?' he asked. 'Luxurious surroundings. Good food. Excellent accommodation. First-rate recreational facilities. And?' – he looked at her – 'attractive companions. When we might be getting our fingernails torn out by the Gestapo. Some might say we are very lucky.'

'Is that what you say?' asked Clare.

Loach stopped playing.

'Listen,' he said. 'I'm only waiting for one thing.'

She waited.

'To get away.'

She said, almost idly:

'Why did they send you here?'

Loach didn't even blink.

'I'll ask you that,' he said smoothly. 'Why you?'

'Ince said . . .' She stopped.

'Major Ince!' said Loach. 'My dear, you are beginning to feel the strain. You are actually being indiscreet. Fancy, Major Ince . . .'

'You know him?'

'Yes,' said Loach. 'I know Major Ince.'

Clare stared at him.

'Your move,' said Loach.

44

When Ince got to his office, the lieutenant with the Royal Berkshire Regiment badges had been waiting twenty minutes.

'Sorry to keep you, Martin,' said Ince. 'It's a Monday Monday today.'

Very rarely Ince made jokes. This was one of them, and he usually said it on Mondays. Very few people laughed. Martin had heard it before, but he gave the feeble smile which satisfied Ince's ego.

'Sit down,' said Ince. 'Now what the hell's all this about?'

'Nothing serious, sir,' said Martin. 'But it needs delicate handling.'

'Well?'

'Chap in the ministry. In Berkeley Square. Political warfare executive type. He's asking questions.'

'Oh, yes,' said Ince. Another bloody politician. 'Can't mind his own business?'

'In a way, it is his business,' said Martin, apologetically.

'Which makes it a bit tricky from security's point of view.'

'What does he want?'

'His name is Gilbert, sir.'

Ince knew what was coming.

'He is asking questions about his daughter.'

'Ah,' said Ince.

'So you see the difficulty,' said Martin, and sat back expectantly.

'Does he know she's with us?' said Ince.

'I think he does, now,' said Martin.

'But how?' said Ince. 'She wouldn't have said anything, I'm sure.'

'We're trying to find out,' said Martin. 'Gilbert has a lot of contact with the Free French. He's over at Duke Street several times a week. He knows Toussaint there.'

'Ah,' said Ince again.

'The point is that he isn't doing any harm yet – but if he keeps on, he might come across something.'

'Warn him off,' said Ince.

'She *is* his daughter,' said Martin. 'He is well connected. He even has the ear of the minister.'

'Him and Glover,' said Ince bitterly.

Glover worked closely with Martin, but the young man gave no hint.

'Hmm,' said Ince Then: 'What is he actually after?'

'He says his daughter seems to have disappeared.'

'Well, tell him she's on active service.'

'Yes, sir,' said Martin.

Ince peered at him.

'You don't approve?'

'No, sir, I think it's a very good idea. I just wanted your go ahead.'

Ince pondered for a moment.

'Are they very close?' he asked.

'Not really,' said Martin. 'But they have been seeing each other. Dinner at the Savoy and all that.'

'Make it convincing,' said Ince. 'If he knows it's us, he must guess what sort of work she's doing.'

'But she isn't of course, sir,' said Martin.

'Yes, Martin, but he doesn't know, does he?' said Ince irritably. If Martin's father hadn't been an ambassador, would the boy ever have been shifted into the department?

'No, of course not, sir,' said Martin. 'As long as all the stories agree.'

'Well, they'd better,' growled Ince. 'Who's going to tell him? You?'

'Oh no, sir,' said Martin. 'He doesn't tie me in with it. Mr Glover will tell him.'

Christ, thought Ince. But he didn't say it.

When Martin had gone, Ince unlocked a drawer in his desk and took out a big envelope. From it he drew a photograph of a girl. A pretty girl. Sylvia.

Ince studied it. He looked sad.

Then he got a portable typewriter, put it on his desk, took off the lid, inserted a sheet of WD foolscap.

He began typing. He only used two fingers, but on the paper it looked neat.

There was no carbon copy. What Ince started to type was so secret that not even his secretary could see it.

45

Colonel Shaw made Clare feel instantly welcome.

'I was wondering how long it would take you to ask,' he said.

She had expected bluff, excuses, maybe even veiled threats about wanting to know too much. Instead, Shaw was full of understanding.

'It's bound to be a bit of a shock to be stuck in a place like this, cut off from everybody and everything,' he said.

'What's the point of it ...' she said, baffled by his reasonableness.

'It's a security problem, Miss Gilbert. We have to handle it rather delicately.'

'I don't understand,' said Clare.

Shaw had been standing by the window of his office. Now he came over, and sat opposite her.

'I won't mince words,' he said. 'You've been compromised.'

He said it very patiently, like a doctor explaining to a patient a little infection which wasn't very serious in itself, but could have grave consequences if it wasn't treated properly.

'Compromised?' said Clare. 'What does that mean?'

'Let me put it this way,' said Shaw, and he slipped into the patter easily, for he was used to it. 'Everybody here is special. They've all been trained for something special. They've all been earmarked for secret jobs on the other side. Hand-picked. Like yourself.'

He smiled at her encouragingly.

'Well, sometimes something goes wrong. Jerry finds out something. He gets a clue. A hint, about a face, a person, a name. It could jeopardize the whole mission. Makes it far too risky to send the person.'

'But who...'

'So when somebody's compromised, like yourself, we whip 'em out of sight. We keep 'em here, hidden away, where nobody knows anything about 'em. We keep 'em on ice. Until it's safe to use 'em.'

'What has this to do with me?' said Clare.

'I know it's a blow,' said Shaw. 'And believe me, it's no reflection on you at all. Nobody suggests you've done anything wrong. People can get compromised the silliest way. Sometimes we're even too cautious. But one mustn't take chances, must one?'

'They never said anything about this,' said Clare. 'Major Ince talked about special training. He never said...'

'Of course not,' said Shaw silkily. 'He's hardly going to shout it from the roof-tops of Portman Square, is he?'

Clare's mouth was dry.

'Who found out about me?' she said.

'Ah,' said Shaw. 'No idea. Need to know, and all that. I don't need to know, you see. They just tell me to look after you till the all-clear's given.'

She shook her head.

'You mean everybody here has been betrayed . . .' she began.

'Compromised,' he said. The word betrayed seemed distasteful.

'Everybody? People like Captain Loach?'

'Oh, Captain Loach,' he said genially. 'How are you two getting on? You seem quite chummy.'

'You can't help it, cooped up here,' said Clare. She fell silent.

'It's not such a bad place, now, is it?' said Shaw. 'And if there is anything you'd like, I'm sure . . .'

'I'd like to get out,' said Clare. 'I want to do the job they've trained me for.'

'You will,' said Shaw. 'You're only here until we get the green light. Then you'll be sent to do a job quickly enough, believe me.'

He was being soothing, comforting, but Clare was still full of fear.

'Can't I do something else meanwhile? Not just this awful boring routine every day?' she pleaded.

'It may be boring,' said Shaw, 'but it's very important. We're keeping you on your toes. All of you. We don't want you to get rusty. You're too valuable to waste.'

She knew then that he would just go on saying it, the same formula, and that it would never sound any different, and that she was trapped.

He saw her look, and lit a cigarette.

'It's frightening,' she said.

'What is?'

'That – somebody's told them. About me. That they know about me. It's not nice, feeling you've been betrayed by a spy.'

Shaw looked interested.

'Who said anything about a spy, Miss Gilbert?' he asked.

'Well, somebody must have found out,' she snapped.

'That's all been taken care of,' he said. 'There's really nothing to worry about.'

Colonel Shaw was a very good liar.

46

Grau spent all the sweet coupons he had left on buying a bar of chocolate for the girl. He liked to bring her a little present when he dropped by in the evening.

Of course he took great care that she did not know much about him. He didn't even give her the Harris name. To her, he was Reece. He lived in digs somewhere in Paddington. He was a commercial traveller. And, curiously enough, he made up a wife. He didn't really know why, except perhaps making out he had a guilt problem helped his relationship with Sylvia.

Grau's problem was that he found himself increasingly drawn to the girl. Physically, she provided him with something for which he had had to hunt in the dark streets and bargain in shop doorways. Emotionally, she was an experience he had not known since he began operating in London – a human being with whom he had a personal contact.

Of course, it was dangerous. All his training told him never to establish a regular link with an outsider. Safety in numbers, always. Security in anonymity. Vanish before they get to know you.

But one had to risk danger when one was on to something big. And Grau knew that Sylvia could be very useful, providing he didn't panic her, and slowly, patiently extracted the little pieces of information which she knew.

That Sylvia had been on the call-girl list of an Intelligence department Grau worked out pretty soon. But what Intelligence department?

Gradually, as they drank together in the evenings, or lay in bed, little snippets came out. About the foreigners she comforted. Frenchmen. And Englishmen who spoke French beautifully. How they didn't wear uniform, but if they did it was all kinds. About trips they were going to make, or journeys from which they had just returned, and would talk about.

Grau didn't know where it would lead. Or what use he could finally make of Sylvia. But she was important enough to be cultivated.

The only thing that made him uneasy was that he enjoyed it. Sometimes, he even relaxed with her. It was – unprofessional. And risky.

But he was human.

'What's your wife like?' asked Sylvia one night, coming in from the bathroom, naked.

'Nothing like you,' said Grau. He thought of the Croxley woman. 'She can be a real cow.'

'That's not very nice of you,' said Sylvia, primly. 'You did marry her.'

'I'm not a very nice man,' said Grau.

She sat on the edge of the bed. Grau had been reading about the Salerno fighting in *The Star*, but the paper fell on the floor, unheeded.

'Stay till morning,' said Sylvia.

'I wish I could,' he muttered.

'What's stopping you?' she said. 'Afraid she'll find out?'

'It's not that easy,' said Grau.

Sometimes she was very drunk. He would find her, sprawling, clutching a half-empty bottle, lipstick smudged, and that vile scar vivid across her face.

And he felt pity for her. Watch it, he said to himself. She's a drunken whore. What's romantic about that?

The radio messages he had sent, composites of things he had picked up from her which tallied with bits he had found out elsewhere, had been received with interest on the other side.

And even Grau, who could only see one small corner of the whole picture, realized that he had stumbled across something valuable.

Once or twice they went out for a meal in a café, or had some fish and chips. Sylvia didn't really care. But for some reason she wanted him.

Then, one day, it seemed to Grau that she was tense and worried. He came in, and she gave him a nervous smile.

Later, she said: 'What do you actually sell, Harry?'

'I told you, I'm a traveller,' he said.

'Yes, but what in?'

He poured himself another glass of beer.

'Why?' he asked.

'Nothing,' she said, 'just curious.'

She was jumpy about the blackout too, and he had never noticed that before.

'Mustn't get the police in here,' she said, with an artificial laugh, drawing the curtains tight.

She *is* on edge, he decided.

'Anything worrying you?' asked Grau casually.

'What should worry me?' she said.

In bed that night, she said suddenly:

'Harry, how are you off?'

'Eh?'

'Have you got some money?'

What would she say if I told I have all the money I could want, as much of it as I want, when I want, he thought.

'Why, do you need any?'

'I might.'

'I can let you have a few quid,' said Grau.

It was strange, because she had been proud, fiercely proud of being independent. The game provided her with a living after all.

During that night, she suddenly clutched him, tight. She was shivering.

'Harry, I'm frightened,' she whispered.

He held her, until she fell asleep. Then, very gently, he got out of bed, dressed, and went into the night.

His instinct told him to stay away. Something had happened.

For some reason, she was jumpy. Grau couldn't understand why, but the warning was there.

So he avoided her for a week, and took no notice of the inner voice which urged him not to drop an invaluable source of information. What was there to panic about?

AMT VII wanted more. They wanted certain things checked out. They had some names they would like him to try on his contact. They would appreciate this, and they needed that.

Maybe Grau would have told them to go to hell, but he did want to see her again.

He had got used to Sylvia, and cursed himself for it.

He bought the bar of chocolate, and took a bus. She always told him to ring three times. It was their signal. And three times he pushed the button. The door opened with a click.

Grau went up the staircase that had become so familiar to him, and was about to knock on her flat door, with the brown paint peeling.

It was ajar. Grau pushed it open, and stepped into the small flat.

'Hallo,' he called out. 'It's me.'

There was no answer, but the light was on in the kitchen.

'Sylvia,' said Grau, and he felt excited anticipation at seeing her.

Sylvia wasn't in the kitchen. But a man was sitting at the table. He nodded amiably to Grau.

'Good evening,' he said. 'Mr Reece?'

Grau froze.

The man got up.

'My name is Ince,' he said. 'Major Ince.'

47

In his nightmare moments, Grau had often wondered what it would be like when it happened.

A tap on the door? Gentle perhaps, almost apologetic. Or a

thunder of footsteps running up the stairs, shouts, a furious banging? Would it happen in broad daylight, in the street – a car suddenly pulling up alongside the kerb, men jumping out, grabbing him? Would there be a gun pointed at him, the click of handcuffs, or would it be very gentlemanly and polite?

But not this way. This was not what he had expected.

He did not need to ask who Ince was. Sylvia had let the name slip. This was them. The organization. He knew what this meant. So he had nothing to lose. He might try a final bluff.

'I was looking for – Miss . . .' said Grau, rather as if he was the window-cleaner or the milkman.

'Sylvia?' said Ince affably. 'She isn't here just now. Why don't you sit down.'

Grau was determined to play the charade to the full.

'Oh, that's all right,' he said. 'I only dropped by on the off-chance. Perhaps you'll tell her I'll be in touch.'

And he turned to leave.

Ince made no move. Instead, he said:

'Do stay, Mr Reece. I'd like a little chat with you.'

There was no threat in his tone. It was almost gentle.

'Oh, yes?' said Grau, carefully.

'You and Sylvia have become great friends, haven't you?' said Ince, waving him to the other kitchen chair.

Maybe he could still bluff it, thought Grau. Maybe.

'Look here,' he said, 'this is all a little embarrassing for me. I mean, if you and she . . .'

He swallowed.

'I do want you to understand that . . . that . . .'

He stopped.

Ince regarded him benignly.

'I do understand, Mr Reece,' he said. 'And I'm sure you do.'

Did he have anybody outside, wondered Grau. Was the house surrounded? Did he have people all over the place? His people, armed?

He tried a different ploy. After all, if they were on to him, it didn't matter. And if they were not, it might still help.

'No, I must explain,' said Grau, playing the little suburban husband anxious to keep his secret. 'Actually, my name isn't Reece.'

'Really?' said Ince.

'No,' gushed Grau. 'It's Harris. Arthur Harris. I'm married, you see.'

Ince nodded, full of understanding.

'And of course, you don't want any problems – with Sylvia. So you call yourself Reece.'

Grau nodded.

'It's so much simpler, all the way round,' he said.

'Quite so,' said Ince.

'So I think I'd better go,' said Grau. 'She'll understand ...'

'I'm sure she will,' said Ince, and added, without changing his manner, 'I wonder if I could see your identity card, Mr Harris.'

Damn, thought Grau. I knew it wouldn't work, but he almost had me fooled.

But he wasn't giving in yet.

'My identity card?' he said, 'why should I show you my identity card?'

'Perhaps you'd rather show it to the police,' said Ince sadly.

'What has the police got to do with it?' said Grau. 'And who are you anyway, Major – Major Ince, or whatever your name is? What business do you have here?'

'Please,' said Ince, and held out his hand.

They both knew they were playing a game now, and Grau knew he had lost it.

He got out his wallet, with its careful selection of bona-fide content, and pulled out his blue identity card with the royal coat of arms.

Ince looked at it, displaying no particular interest.

'Arthur James Harris' he read to himself, while Grau watched fascinated. 'ABPQ stroke 113 stroke 1. Ah yes. Is that your national registration number? And address?'

'Of course, it is,' said Grau.

'Thank you very much,' said Ince, and pocketed the identity card.

'I need that,' said Grau.

'I don't think you will any more,' said Ince gently.

He stood up.

'I think you know who I am, Mr Harris,' he said. 'We'll find a taxi, shall we?'

I must be crazy, thought Grau. Is this it? The arrest?

'I don't know what you're talking about,' said Grau. 'And I want my identity card.'

Ince sighed.

'We're both professionals, aren't we?' he said. 'At least I am, and I think you are. But I can make it formal if you like. All right?'

They left the flat, and Ince slammed the front door shut.

Outside, Ince looked up and down the street, for a cab.

Grau, beside him, thought: this is madness. It just can't be like this.

For a fleeting moment, he thought of taking to his heels, disappearing round the corner. But what was the point?

Out of the shadows, a young man in a raincoat had joined them. He must have been hanging around all the time.

'Everything all right, sir?' the young man asked Ince respectfully.

'Splendid, Martin, everything's splendid,' said Ince. He beamed at Grau: 'Isn't it, Mr Harris?'

Then he said to the young man:

'I do wish you'd find us a cab. Mr Harris is shivering.'

48

Loach had become secretive. He went for long walks by himself, exploring the sprawling grounds of the place, probing just how far one was allowed to roam at Inverloch.

Once he came face to face, unexpectedly, with one of the green-bereted Commandos. That didn't worry Loach so much as the Alsatian the man was holding by a tight leash.

'Lost your way, sir?' asked the Commando politely.

'Just getting some air,' said Loach, lightly.

'That's the way back, sir,' said the Commando, very correct. It was not so much a helpful direction as an order.

Loach did not just spend his time exploring. Furtively, he drew a map of the layout. He looked in the library for a local guide, in vain, of course. At night, he studied the stars and their position.

Clare suspected what was going on. She was the only one with whom Loach had established any kind of intimacy. He had made no secret with her that he wanted to get away.

'But what will you do then?' she asked him, once.

'Get to London.'

'And then?'

He only smiled.

'Go and see the Section – tell Major Ince you're fed up being stuck in this hole?'

'Major Ince,' said Loach, 'is the last person I'll go to.'

And he wouldn't say any more.

After Clare had seen Shaw, he tried to extract every word the colonel had said to her. It was like a debriefing. But Clare would only say so much, and no more.

'You mean he told you there's a reason we're all here?' asked Loach.

She nodded.

'But what?'

'Why don't you ask him yourself?' said Clare, and he realized yet again, as he was often conscious, that he could not trust her.

Any more than she could trust him.

After that, Loach was seen less. He would appear at meal-times, and at lectures or discussion groups, nod, sit through it, and then disappear again.

One evening he was a little more talkative.

'You realize nobody knows we're in here,' he suddenly said to Clare.

'Of course,' she said.

'As far as next of kin are concerned, we're doing the job we were going to do all along,' he said, almost to himself.

'I suppose so.'

'And they don't really have to account for us,' said Loach. 'Because we are on active service.'

Clare said nothing.

'Only they think we're on some secret job on the continent. And what would happen if we got killed?'

'Nobody's going to get killed,' said Clare. She wasn't quite sure if she sounded convincing.

'No,' said Loach.

He smiled at her.

'I hope not. You're much too pretty.'

He looked at his watch.

'I think I'll go for a walk,' he announced.

'It's getting late,' said Clare.

'Not for me,' said Loach, and went off.

Within the self-contained world of Inverloch, there was no curfew.

So when Loach entered his room shortly before 2 AM, having done some exploring on the estate, nobody challenged him at any point.

He closed the door, and sat down on his bed.

Perhaps he was looking for a sign. Or perhaps somebody had been careless, and Loach's in-built alarm system switched on.

But he did not have to look round for long to realize that while he had been out, his room had been searched.

Very thoroughly searched.

It was just bad luck for them that they had shifted the thread that Loach had placed on the small desk, as a routine precaution, one end held down by a small cuff-link box, the other by his bottle of after-shave.

Loach would probably have noticed that the room had been

searched anyway. He had been well trained to be on the look-out for such things, and he also had a good instinct anyway for signs of danger.

He had no illusions that it had not been a thorough and professional research. What they hadn't found, of course, was the thing in which they would have been very interested.

The thing that he had been carrying on him while they were looking in here.

His very detailed and accurate little hand-drawn map of the Cooler.

49

Grau looked round the bedroom, and felt he could have done worse. It compared quite favourably with what Mrs Croxley offered him.

The only trouble was that if he opened the door, one of the men would be sitting there in the armchair, doing a crossword puzzle, reading *Punch*, or dozing.

Dozing, that is, until Grau opened the door. Then he'd be very awake.

One of the men was always around Grau now. For somebody like him, who had been living in the anonymity of loneliness, isolated, and detached, this was difficult to accept. But he had no choice.

Life had changed completely anyway. From Sylvia's flat, he was taken to what had been a school in Hammersmith. There, in the study where a housemaster once disciplined erring school-boys, he had undergone five hours of interrogation.

That was on the first night.

Next day, the barrage of questions continued.

Now they knew who he was. What he did. Where he came from. What he was after.

He had not made it difficult for them, and they had been reasonably pleasant. From the start, Grau had accepted the inevitable. As soon as they checked on Arthur James Harris, ABPQ 113/1, the game was over. And it would not take a genius to find the radio in the bookshop.

So he admitted it all.

It was on the second day that he began to wonder if, after all, he might escape the hangman yet. For although he was a prisoner, nobody had put him under arrest. And although they knew he was a spy, nobody charged him.

And they were deceptively kind. They asked him if he preferred tea or coffee. To his surprise, he was given a copy of the *Daily Mirror* every morning. He was provided with some anti-acid powder for his nervous stomach, and they asked him if he wanted anything special, like his regular brand of cigarettes, or was there an author whose books he liked.

He was never alone, of course. Sometimes he did not see the man who was his shadow, but he could feel him, outside the bathroom door, in the next room, in the corridor. He could establish no link with this man, whoever he was. He did not know his name, or anything about him. Just when his face began to be familiar, another one took over for the day, or the evening.

Then they took Grau to his flat. Mrs Croxley was shaken when her missing lodger stood there, with three very polite men. They packed all her lodger's things, paid her a month's rent, locked her out of the room while they searched every inch of it, and then told her she had a vacancy. Mr Harris would not be back.

'What is all this about, Mr Harris?' said the Croxley woman. 'Who are these men?'

'Colleagues of mine,' said Grau, and in a way he was perfectly right.

'You've got to give me proper notice,' said Mrs Croxley. 'You can't just get out like this. You owe me legal notice.'

That's when one of the men gave her the money.

'One month's rent,' he said genially. 'Perhaps you could give Mr Harris a receipt.'

'After all I've done for you,' said Mrs Croxley. She turned to the three men.

'He's been treated like one of the family,' she said indignantly. 'Washed his shirts, and alway had a snack for him when he wanted it. You wouldn't think anything was rationed.'

'Have we got everything?' one of the men asked Grau politely.

Mrs Croxley looked at Grau grimly.

'Wait till I tell my son,' she said. 'He'll have something to say, walking out like this.'

Grau was slightly puzzled that they had said nothing to Mrs Croxley, not who they were, or why they were taking him away, or what it was all about. He wondered why she had not been taken off for questioning herself – how long have you known this man, how did he become your lodger, did you notice anything unusual about him, did he have any callers?

'I suppose you're going to move in with your fancy bit,' said Mrs Croxley. She had never forgiven Grau for the nights he stayed with Sylvia. She didn't know who it was, but she suspected the worst.

'Have you got his ration book?' one of the men asked Mrs Croxley.

'He does his own shopping,' she sniffed.

'Of course,' said the man.

Mrs Croxley was quite red with fury.

'Cat got your tongue?' she said to Grau. 'Can't even say thank you for all I've done?'

Grau looked at her with distaste. But he wasn't going to give anything away.

'I'm sorry,' he said, 'I didn't expect this, actually. I've had – a change of plans.'

'You owe me for the milk,' said Mrs Croxley. 'And there's a shirt in the wash.'

'That's all right,' said Grau. 'It'll all be settled.'

'Ready?' asked one of the men.

'What is the forwarding address?' asked Mrs Croxley haughtily.

'We'll look after all that,' said the man, but did not explain.

'I'll have my keys,' said Mrs Croxley.

They had taken everything from Grau, but one of the men had them. He handed them over to Mrs Croxley, who seemed surprised that he was the one to produce the key-ring. She would have been even more surprised if she had known that they had already cut a replica set. Just in case.

In the lift down, Grau could not resist saying:

'She knows absolutely nothing.'

It wasn't a chivalrous attempt to keep Mrs Croxley clear of the business. It was more a statement of pride that he had successfully kept the bitch completely in the dark.

One of the three men allowed himself a smile.

'That I can well believe,' he said.

50

Clare could see the girl again, facing her, only this time the roles were reversed. It was Margit who was the aggressor, rushing forward, hatred on her face, her fingers curved like talons. Clare retreated, but Margit was on her, one claw in her hair, the other going for her eyes, her face. It was a wild ferocious struggle, and suddenly Clare knew fear. She was fighting for her life, and it became a silent, ruthless battle, both women trying to kill, and Clare aware that she could not survive.

Now they were locked in each other's arms, swaying like lovers in some lesbian orgy, two women, breast to breast, pressing against each other, only the passion was hatred. Suddenly Margit had her hands round Clare's throat. Desperately Clare tried to fight back, but the hands that beat against the other girl had no power. She raised a knee, trying to kick Margit in the stomach, but it was too late, Margit's hands were tighter and tighter, Clare was gasping for air, the breath of life was being choked out of her, and Margit was smiling triumphantly and it all exploded . . .

That was when Clare woke up, and the shock that she had only dreamt it did not bring any real relief. She felt exhausted, and her eyes were heavy. Clare had gone to bed naked, and her body was damp with perspiration. So were the bedclothes.

In the dark, she reached out for the glass of water by her bedside. It was luke-warm, but she took sip after sip, as if it was a medicine that would cure all. The nightmare was not a new one. Only sometimes the woman who tried to kill her wasn't the Polish girl, but the blonde mistress her father planned to marry, the woman who had usurped her mother's place, and it was in those dreams that Clare not only felt fury at being the one who was losing the fight, but regret that she could not kill the other one.

She looked at her watch. Just after 3.15 AM. All she could hear was the steady, unhurried tick of a grandfather clock that stood in the corridor near her room. The clock must have been there when the lairds ruled this little kingdom, and it had never been moved. Now it was still ticking away, undisturbed by the curious secrets of the new masters of Inverloch.

Clare closed her eyes. If only she could sleep. She would give a lot to find that when she looked at her watch again it was seven, and time to get up, and another four hours had ticked away. Perhaps a sleeping pill . . .

But that was out of the question. The place had a dispensary, and even a small sickbay with four beds. The doctor, a captain in the Royal Army Medical Corps, seemed friendly, and there would be no problem. But Clare wasn't going to start that. No sleeping pills.

Not that she would be the only one to rely on their comfort. Inverloch was very easy-going that way. There didn't even seem to be any difficulty about drink for those who needed its solace. Clare had watched the Dutchman, for example, relying more and more on his brandy.

At least, she thought he was Dutch. He had that sort of

accent, and he looked like a Dutchman. Which, she knew, was ridiculous, because what does a Dutchman look like?

When she first arrived, he nodded politely to her if they happened to sit near each other, or to meet during the day. Gradually, however, he had become more and more withdrawn. Then, one evening, Clare realized that the Dutchman was drunk. Not wildly so, but sufficiently to have to pronounce every word with great care.

She had no idea where he got drunk each day, even as it became clearer that this was now a permanent state. Until she met him going up to his room, carrying a virgin bottle of brandy.

She saw him a couple of days later, again with a new bottle. It was still wrapped in tissue paper.

And he had just come out of the dispensary.

Clare was quite right. The RAMC doctor was not just there to look after physical aches and pains. If certain aids were needed to help a person accept the hospitality of the Cooler, the taxpayer would provide it. As a medicinal service, of course.

So sleeping pills would really be no problem at all.

51

They had visited the bookshop, and Grau had shown them the radio, and then they had a long day while he explained to them his transmission schedules, and the message pattern, and exactly how he communicated with Reinecke.

They didn't tell Grau too much, but he had a shrewd suspicion that they did not just take his word for these things. And he was right. They carefully checked the dates and times and sequences that he gave them against the log of the interception stations who had for long noted every illicit radio transmission for which Grau had been responsible.

He still had no idea what they were going to do with him. He knew the technique would be to assign one 'father figure' to him, on whom he could rely, or at least they hoped he would, whom he could ask questions, and who could reassure him about things that mattered.

He suspected their Major Ince was just that. But he wasn't sure. That was why he knew how skilled they were. They used uncertainty and doubt like a violin, playing every variation of the theme to make him feel insecure without frightening him into the kind of panic that would make him useless.

Not once had there been any ideological questions.

Nobody had asked how do you feel about Hitler, or are you a Nazi supporter, or what do you think of the Jews, or what are your thoughts about the Third Reich?

Clearly they accepted him as a professional. And you don't ask a practising dentist why he pulls teeth.

About noon, Ince came to him.

'Well, how are you settling in, Mr Harris?' he asked.

Ince still used the Harris name, which Grau found amusing. But this bland concern for his comfort was becoming a bit too much. What did he mean by settling in, anyway? What had he settled into?

'I'm being very well treated,' said Grau carefully.

Ince nodded. 'Good.'

'But how long is this going to last?'

Ince appeared surprised.

'Is anything the matter?' he asked, innocently.

'Only that I want to know what will happen – to me,' said Grau. 'I'm sure you understand.'

'Let's have lunch,' was all Ince said.

Grau still did not know where they were actually keeping him. After the school in Hammersmith, he was taken to a house in Regent's Park, near Avenue Road, for some more questioning. Then they brought him to this place. But it was dark at the time. His impression was of a Victorian house that had seen better times. Somewhere in Kensington?

Grau had been having all his meals in the house, and he did not expect to be taken anywhere. It was also the first time that he did not have one of his shadows.

Outside, a small plain car was waiting. Ince drove, and Grau sat beside him. As they swung out of the street, into the main road, Grau caught sight of the name: 'Addison Road'.

There was a question Grau had wanted to ask for a long time. As they stopped at some traffic lights, he decided to try it.

'What has happened to Sylvia?' he asked.

Ince let out the clutch.

'She's well,' he said.

'Not in any trouble?' asked Grau, picking his words carefully.

Ince slowed down behind a bus.

'Good Lord, no. Why should she be?'

'I wondered . . .' said Grau.

'You mean, are we annoyed with her? Of course not.'

'She didn't really give anything away,' said Grau. He was determined to do what he could.

Ince accelerated.

'Even if she did, she did us a good service,' he said.

'Oh?'

Ince looked at him sideways, beaming.

'You, Mr Harris. That was a very good service.'

But she couldn't have betrayed him, Grau thought, as he had done so many times since they had found him. She didn't know anything to betray. Did she?

'She was not involved,' said Grau.

'Don't worry about Sylvia,' said Ince, and neatly cut up an American staff car at Marble Arch.

In Oxford Street, Ince said:

'We're going to a little restaurant you might enjoy. It'll make a change anyway, from all that home cooking.'

How absurd, thought Grau. Here they were driving through London traffic, a German spy caught by British Intelligence, and the man who was softening him up. They might be old friends, or business associates. Perhaps even school chums. Hardly the hunted and the hunter. Or the victim and his executioner.

Ince parked in Charlotte Street.

'I hope this is to your taste,' he said, and took Grau across the road to Schmidt's.

Inside, Ince went straight to a table at which a man was already sitting. The man stood up, smiling.

'Good to see you, Ince,' he said. His eyes pierced Grau. 'Mr Harris.'

'This is Mr Smith,' said Ince. He did not even try to make Smith sound credible.

And he certainly did not tell Grau that the man was a lieutenant-colonel, and that to the Joint Intelligence Committee and to the Directorate of Special Intelligence and to the committee whose work was so secret that even its initials were unknown except to its members, he was known as Deception.

'I've been studying the menu, gentlemen,' said Deception, 'and it is up to standard. Mr Schmidt does not let us down.'

Like the perfect host, he put the menu in front of Grau.

'Have you been here before, Mr Harris?' asked Ince, quite innocent.

'It's not one of my haunts,' said Grau, wondering what the sauerkraut would be like. Sarcastic bastards, picking this place.

Deception nodded.

'Actually, it proves how much more civilized everybody's become,' he said. 'In the last war, they would have had their windows smashed. Now nobody cares.'

'But didn't they have a sign up saying "Swiss ex-servicemen"?' asked Ince.

'Isn't it absurd how these stories get around,' said Deception, and proceeded to order goulash from the sullen waiter.

It was a meal during which Grau concentrated very little on his food.

Especially after Deception's opening remark.

'I hear you've been very helpful, Mr Harris,' he said.

Grau shrugged.

'In my position . . .'

Deception wiped his mouth carefully with the serviette.

'Of course, you could be still more helpful,' he said.

'I have answered all the questions,' said Grau. 'But if there is anything I haven't...'

'Mr Smith does not mean more questions,' said Ince, his eyes watching Grau.

'You see,' said Deception, 'there are two things you can do, Mr Harris. You can hang yourself.'

Grau felt cold.

'I mean, we would do the hanging, of course. Only it would be you who puts the rope round your neck.'

Grau stayed silent.

'That's number one. But then that's foolish talk. Much more helpful is the other alternative. Helpful to you. And us. And Germany.'

That took Grau by surprise. Helpful to Germany?

'You're in an impossible situation, Mr Harris, we all know that,' said Deception. 'But you're a good German and you want to help your country. As I want to help mine. To end the war quickly, so that we don't lose millions more of our countrymen.'

Ince was studying the wallpaper behind Grau's head.

'So, if you help us, you will be doing the patriotic thing,' said Deception, and he sat back like the teacher who has clearly demonstrated an irrefutable mathematical law.

'I have told you all I can,' said Grau. His voice was low.

It was Ince's turn now.

'We want you to carry on as before,' he said, leaning forward confidentially. 'We want you to keep in touch with your people, and continue to supply them with information. Just as you have been doing.'

Grau sat rigid.

'And we will be giving you the information,' said Deception.

'You're making life very difficult for yourself,' said the assistant governor.

Sylvia, in her drab prison frock, looked at the woman with distaste. What a boring creature.

'You should really settle down, and try to make the best of it,' said the assistant governor. 'We cannot help you if you won't knuckle down.'

Knuckle down, you bitch, thought Sylvia. That's your kind of talk all right.

'I know you've had a hard time,' said the assistant governor. 'Things have not been easy for you. Now take your punishment, and when you come out, I'm sure the court missionary or the welfare society will try and find you something. Perhaps a domestic job.'

Sylvia spat at the assistant governor.

Right in her face. Her aim was excellent.

It was some sort of consolation as she was half-dragged and half-carried by three women prison warders to the punishment cell. One of them gave her a couple of hard punches in the kidneys, and another kicked her before the door was slammed on her, but Sylvia didn't mind. The sight of the spittle beginning to run down the assistant governor's fat, shiny face almost made up for all the pain and aches.

She had been framed, she knew that.

She knew it would happen after Ince had descended on her, and she had had to explain why she had not made herself available to them, ignored messages, and why she was spending her time with the curious Mr Reece.

And what had Mr Reece wanted from her? What had he asked her, they wanted to know. What had she told him? How did she meet him? Why was he so interested in her?

'He likes me,' she had sobbed.

The raised eyebrow drove her mad.

'He likes to fuck me,' she screamed.

And then she admitted that she had talked about the things she had done. And the people she had done them for. People like Captain Loach.

'And what did you say about Captain Loach?' Ince asked softly.

She had told him.

After that it was only a matter of time.

She was not even surprised when they arrested her, and charged her with stealing an American sailor's wallet, which they found in her handbag. She had never seen it before, but beside the detective sergeant stood a smooth young man, and she could guess where he was from.

She had enough convictions for soliciting, but a good lawyer could have argued that Sylvia had never been guilty of dishonesty in her life, and stealing was completely uncharacteristic of her. The sailor, of course, wasn't in court, and really, it wasn't a very stirring case.

But just before she came up in court, Ince visited her in the cells.

'I'm sorry to hear about this trouble,' he said. 'I had no idea...'

'Haven't you?'

'Of course not. The reason I came is merely to remind you that under the provisions of the Official Secrets Act...'

She laughed wryly.

'Don't worry. I know.'

'I hope it won't be too unpleasant,' he said. 'You should be out by autumn...'

As they led her into court, she was still wondering whether to fight it. Yet she knew, all the time, that she was really beaten. What was the point? They'd only get her for something else, in another place. Perhaps something even more unpleasant. Perhaps even dangerous. Sherlock Mews had her trapped, one way or the other.

So when she faced the court, and they asked her how she pleaded, she looked straight at the magistrate and said:

'Guilty.'

She got six months. Ince had been right. By autumn she should be out.

But until then she was indeed very much out of the way.

In a place where she could not talk.

Sylvia, alone in the dark punishment cell, sat and sobbed.

53

Grau who had been Harris who had been Reece became Oscar.

That was the name Deception gave him. And only Deception used it.

To the rest, he remained Harris.

As Oscar, he had been turned.

Grau accepted the fact with realism. He had no choice, and as long as he was alive ...

He also knew that nobody had told him everything. Somewhere along the line, there were others, but whose side he had no idea. The question of whether he should be true to his new masters was largely academic. His shadows were constantly around him. They knew what he ate, what he read, how he slept.

Not always, perhaps, what he thought. Sometimes he wasn't even sure about that. They would confront him with a piece of information, quite innocent in itself, which he had never guessed they knew about, and he would explain. They clearly did it not so much because they were interested in that particular thing, but to show him that nothing escaped them.

That he could have no secrets from them.

They continued to use the bookshop for the transmissions. It clearly pleased their sense of artistry that the same set, in the same premises, should be used. They were tense during the first two or three transmissions, but after a few days they suddenly relaxed. It almost seemed as if they had had confirmation from across the water that Grau's messages were still considered authentic.

To the biggest question of all, they already knew the answer. It pleased Grau that he only had to confirm it, not betray it.

'It's the landing, isn't it?' asked Ince.

'What should I say?'

'We know anyway,' said Ince. 'The key to your operation. Time, date, and place of the invasion.'

'There have been other things,' said Grau. 'Troop build-ups. That curious 2nd Army that doesn't exist and yet it does. Whether it's real or not. The agents you are sending across with the final instructions. Yes, you're right. It all comes down to one thing. The invasion.'

'Any idea?' asked Ince casually.

Grau liked that. The man had charm.

'My dear Major, how could I know?'

'You've been busy enough,' said Ince. 'I wonder if you've formed your own conclusions.'

'I look at the map,' said Grau. 'And I say to myself Pas de Calais.'

'Quite right too,' said Ince.

Grau was startled.

'You mean I am correct?'

'I mean I think the same thing.'

'You know it?'

Ince shook his head.

'They tell very few people,' he said.

'Of whom you are one,' pressed Grau. He was feeling reckless.

'You must think I am much more important than I am,' said Ince.

Grau smiled.

'I don't think you're exactly as important as you make out, Major,' he said.

A few days later, Grau insisted on seeing Ince urgently.

'I have to send a private message to Germany,' he said.

'Private,' said Ince, almost lazily.

'Yes, quite personal,' said Grau.

'I see,' said Ince.

'You must trust me,' said Grau.

'Just how private will private be?' asked Ince.

'You can read it,' said Grau. 'But it won't make sense to you.'

'Try me.'

'No, you will understand it, but you will still think it is a trick. That is why you must trust me.'

'What's the message?' said Ince.

'Birthday greetings to my mother,' said Grau.

Ince was quite unmoved.

'I see,' he said.

'I always send her birthday greetings,' said Grau. 'Wherever I am.'

'Bit risky, isn't it?' said Ince softly.

'I am very fond of my mother,' said Grau.

'When do you have to send it?' inquired Ince.

'Tomorrow,' said Grau. 'Otherwise I miss her birthday.'

'That would never do,' said Ince.

He talked it over with Deception.

'He could be trying it on,' said Deception.

'If he's tired of living,' said Ince.

'On the other hand, agents are strange people. Family ties matter to them almost more. Where does she live?'

'Bad Homburg.'

'We've got somebody in Frankfurt who could check up – it's only a few miles,' mused Deception.

'By tomorrow? Hardly time, is it. And do you want to risk a man for that?'

'To catch Oscar double-crossing I'd risk more,' said Deception. 'But maybe you're right. It's a bit short notice.'

Then he brightened.

'I'll tell you something. Let's check the interception log. If there was something sent on tomorrow's date last year, in

Oscar's code, we know what it is. And that he's telling the truth.'

Interception did have the signal logged.

'All right,' said Ince to Grau. 'Send her happy birthday.'

'Thank you,' said Grau.

But the message he encoded was not happy birthday. It said: 'Will see you this time next year.'

'What the hell is this?' said Ince.

'She's getting on,' said Grau. 'I just want to cheer her up. I've sent her happy birthday every year. Now I want her to have something to look forward to.'

'And your people will pass it on to her?'

Grau nodded.

'Colonel Reinecke is very good that way. He cares about the morale of his people in the field.'

The message went off during a routine transmission, part of Grau's scheduled pattern.

It was acknowledged.

When they drove Grau home from the bookshop, he was very cheerful. His shadow noted that he actually whistled through his teeth.

54

Ince was rung in the middle of the night at his flat at Lancaster Gate, and asked to come to the office.

The colonel was already there.

'Here,' said the colonel, and handed Ince a pink slip of paper.

It was a radio intercept by security monitoring.

The message, decoded, read:

'STAND BY 24-HOURLY.'

'Well?' said Ince. He was not feeling at his best, and in his hurry he had put on two odd socks. Ince hated that sort of thing.

'It's to Oscar's Section,' said the colonel. 'Using Oscar's code.'

'But Oscar has no transmission scheduled,' said Ince.

'Exactly,' said the colonel.

Ince stared at the message as if it could unfold hidden secrets.

'Stand by 24-hourly,' he read to himself.

'It's obviously to alert them to expect a message at any time day or night,' said the colonel. 'Outside any planned schedule.'

'Christ,' said Ince. Then:

'Where is he?'

'Tucked up nice and safe in Addison Road,' said the colonel. 'Deception has already checked. They were on to it first thing. You can imagine.'

'They must be expecting to have something big, to go on 24-hours transmission alert,' said Ince.

'Security coordination is meeting first thing in the morning,' said the colonel. 'But we've got trouble anyway.'

'Yes,' said Ince.

'No, not just the message,' said the colonel.

Ince put the paper down on his desk.

'What trouble?'

'It's not only Oscar's code, sent to Oscar's Section. It's where it came from.'

'Sir?'

'Interception say the message came from Inverloch.'

Ince looked blank. The man was raving.

'That signal was transmitted from inside the Cooler,' said the colonel.

'They can't possibly . . .'

'They've pin-pointed it,' said the colonel. 'Inside.'

'Christ,' said Ince, again.

'And you know what that means,' said the colonel.

He knew only too well.

55

They flew Shaw down from Scotland, and as soon as he arrived at Bovington, a staff car rushed him into London.

With him came the bald man, and within half an hour they were in the meeting the colonel had called.

'They have an agent inside the Cooler,' said the colonel.

'Not an agent, sir,' Ince corrected him. 'A traitor. I don't think they've got one of their own people inside. Only somebody working for them.'

'I've done nothing so far,' said Shaw, 'as instructed. Not even a search for the radio.'

The colonel nodded.

'Plenty of time for that,' he said.

'Any idea who it is?' asked the bald man.

'Perhaps,' said Ince.

He savoured the silence that followed.

'Oh?' said Shaw.

'Well, you know why they're there,' said Ince. 'They know too much. They're all people with a load of secrets, agents trained for special assignments, who for some reason or another we can't risk sending on their job. They've revealed a flaw.

'And because they know the faces and the names and the orders of the others, they have to be kept hidden away.

'They don't want to be there. They get put inside because we've discovered something about them we didn't know. A man drinks too much. He talks too much. He can't keep his hands off women.'

'Or he beats somebody up because he can't help it, or goes berserk,' said Shaw. 'Don't I know it.'

'I think we're aware of all this, Ince,' said the colonel, a little impatiently.

'Yes, sir,' said Ince. 'But we've always assumed they didn't want to be in the Cooler. I think our friend is somebody who is quite the opposite. He wanted very much to become one of the select few. He did everything he could to make sure we'd put him in.'

'But why?' said the bald man.

'Because everybody inside has a secret. It's a rich harvesting ground. And they're all people who, one way or another, might give away the secret, perhaps without realizing it. Otherwise, they wouldn't be in the place.'

'Especially one certain secret?' said Shaw.

Ince nodded. 'Exactly.'

The colonel looked at the 1944 calendar on his desk. It was May.

'Yes, time is running out. They must be getting very anxious.'

Shaw smiled grimly.

'If you're right, they're very smart. They have managed to make us put one of their people right into it.'

'They are very smart,' said Ince.

'You say you think you know who it might be?' pressed the bald man.

The buzzer went, and the colonel picked up the phone. He nodded to the others.

'Yes?' he said. 'Good. Send him right in.'

They had fallen silent.

'Carry on, gentlemen,' said the colonel. 'Somebody was delayed.'

Then the door opened, and Deception came in.

'I'm sorry,' he said, 'it's turned into one of those days.'

'Major Ince has just been holding forth on his theory,' said the colonel. 'That somebody deliberately got himself put into the Cooler to find out what he can there.'

Deception nodded.

'And he was about to tell us who it might be,' said the bald man.

'No,' said Ince. 'I'm still working on that. I just have a vague idea.'

'Two names?' said Deception.

'Two names,' said Ince. 'Two possibles.'

'Ah,' said Deception, and seemed satisfied.

For a moment, the others felt like outsiders.

The colonel cleared his throat.

'What about this radio transmission from your place?' he asked Shaw.

'Well,' said Shaw, 'I'm sure you appreciate that the kind of people we've got in there are experts in clandestine radio work. They've all been trained to rig up a wireless transmitter secretly, and send messages under the nose of the Gestapo.'

'Only this time we seem to be the Gestapo,' said the bald man. Deception gave him a cold look.

'It's Oscar's code, acknowledged by Oscar's Section,' said the colonel. 'Any views?'

'I don't think we need to shoot Oscar yet,' said Deception.

He and Ince again exchanged looks, two boys in on the same secret.

'Do you think that whoever is the operator in the Cooler will expect us to react?'

'Put it this way,' said Ince. 'They won't be unprepared for that eventuality.'

'So the next step is . . .' said the colonel.

'I think we should put somebody inside ourselves. To help Major Ince sort out his suspicions, if nothing else,' said Deception.

'How do you feel about that?' the colonel asked Shaw.

'It's your operation, sir,' said Shaw.

'Well?' said the colonel.

'I think I have somebody who might fit in very well,' said Ince.

'From our Section?'

'He's worked with us,' said Ince.

'Who's that?' asked the colonel.

'Actually, I asked him to wait. He's on call outside.'

'That's a little unorthodox,' said the bald man. He prided himself on being a security expert and he felt the whole thing was really slipping out of his hands.

'We have very little time,' said the colonel soothingly. 'I think you'd better call your man in.'

Ince went out, and they sat in uneasy silence. Only Deception seemed perfectly at ease. The colonel thought this kind of game was far too messy. The bald man was annoyed, and Shaw felt they were moving him like a chess piece.

Ince came back, with a young officer in uniform, with Royal Berkshire Regiment insignia.

'This way, Martin,' said Ince.

He led the officer into the room.

'I think some of you gentlemen know Martin,' said Ince.

'You know what this is all about?' asked the colonel.

'I have an idea, sir,' said Martin.

'Good,' said the colonel.

'I'm afraid, Martin,' said Ince, 'that you're about to go into the Cooler.'

No one was smiling.

56

Loach made his escape bid from the Cooler shortly after eleven o'clock at night. He walked into the grounds, as if he intended to take a short stroll before bed.

And he kept going.

He kept to side tracks and narrow paths in the wood, which he had explored during his various reconnaissance trips.

He had put on a warm turtle-neck sweater, and he had thick wool socks. Also, he had made a point of wearing gloves. It was a fine, warm night, but he knew that he would have to brush aside branches and thick bushes in his trek. He did not want his hands cut and scratched.

Loach had prepared in other ways. He had his home-made map, and a small pocket compass he had managed to secrete.

He knew that he should avoid the lanes and country roads that criss-crossed the Inverloch estate. If he could make his route across the acres of wild, desolate parkland without running into a patrol, he might yet get to the road that finally led to the outside world. And then, hopefully, to a village, or even the small railway station, or a main highway. It meant many miles to cover, and many hours ahead, but if he could just avoid being spotted now . . .

Loach calculated that, with luck, he had about seven hours before they realized that he had gone. The fact that he had gone for a walk would not attract any attention. He had, after all, carefully built up that pattern. They would see nothing unusual in it.

And there was no reason why they should be aware that he wasn't in his room. He had deliberately kept awake on three separate nights to find out if, at any time, somebody checked the rooms. But nobody came all night. The bedroom door never opened.

In the morning, he knew, it would take very little time for the alarm to be given. He wondered exactly what they would do next. Send out search parties, and comb the grounds, no doubt. Alert the guards at the gates.

He suspected it wouldn't stop at that. Probably the civilian police would be told. Just what he couldn't guess, but he was sure they had a contingency plan. They would hardly say 'One of our people has escaped'. Or perhaps they would put it in such a way that it made sense. Like, 'An officer in custody has absconded'.

Not that they had to explain anything. The whole area was out of bounds, restricted property under the Defence Regulations. The nearest cottage was probably miles away, and if people ever talked about Inverloch, they would dismiss it as a military place 'where they do secret work'.

Somebody must have tried to get away before, Loach reasoned. He wondered what had happened – being a realist, he did not question that they'd been caught.

And taken back to the Cooler?

At least, he hoped that was all that had happened to them.

After all, who would question anything? A shot, or a body floating in the loch? Who was there to make it public? Who could tell anyone?

Suddenly Loach heard it.

A soft humming noise. Almost like a purr.

He froze. This was no rustling in the trees, no breeze in the wood. This was a dynamo. Here? In the middle of the wilderness of Inverloch?

Cautiously, Loach edged forward. He moved from tree to tree, and the humming grew a little louder. And then he saw it.

A big Army trailer. And next to it, a van, with an aerial on top. A familiar kind of aerial, about which Loach had been carefully coached. A dim light came from the inside of the van. Somebody was in it, and the trailer housed the dynamo.

Loach did not need to see the Royal Corps of Signals insignia to know what he had found. This was a radio surveillance unit. They were monitoring. The aerial was a direction-finder.

And he knew what they were monitoring. The house.

The secret listeners, hidden in their concealed van, had no idea of the curious eyes that were studying their little operation.

Loach melted into the shadows. So. A listening watch. He smiled. The place was full of surprises. But he had something more urgent to do. He had to get away.

And he knew if he did not manage it now, he would never succeed.

He turned, and spotted the jeep. It obviously belonged to the radio unit, but was parked some distance away. Cautiously Loach approached it.

The key was in the ignition. They were careless. For a moment, he considered jumping into the driver's seat, and racing off. It would give him mobility, and speed. With luck, he might cover more distance in an hour than he could all night on foot.

Then he thought again. They would be bound to hear the engine start. And even if they didn't, somebody would soon hear the sound of him racing through the night. At the moment, time was on his side. He could race on unhindered. Once they knew he was on the run . . .

They were bound to be in touch with the duty officer in the house. And with the outlying guard posts. Maybe even with the patrols. Probably by two-way radio. The alarm would be flashed in a minute.

No, it was better resist the temptation. He took stock, and checked his compass. He wanted to go south by south-east. That way, he figured out, would bring him eventually out of the estate.

Loach pressed on. He moved silently, but at as fast a jog-trot as the terrain would allow. The humming from the dynamo receded in the distance. He was alone once more.

He crossed a path, and then made his way across some open land. In the darkness he did not cast a shadow, and he made little noise. He was breathing steadily. His foot broke a twig, and it made a little report, but he did not pause. He wanted to get on.

By now he was four or five miles from the house, deep in the wildness of the Inverloch estate. And it would be quite a few hours before they would realize he had slipped through their fingers.

Now it was slightly uphill, and it needed more effort to keep up the pace. But he was in good shape, and the knowledge that he had to get away helped to whip him on.

'I think you're lost, sir,' said a voice.

Then a bright light blinded him.

He stopped. He raised his hands to his eyes. The light was dazzling him.

'Stay where you are, sir,' said the voice.

The light was lowered slightly, and he saw three men. In uniform. With berets. Marine Commandos. Two of them were keeping him covered with Sten-guns. The third, a sergeant, had a pistol holster, but he hadn't drawn his gun.

'I'm just going for a walk,' said Loach.

'Yes, sir,' said the sergeant politely.

He walked over to Loach.

'Would you mind, sir,' he said, and indicated that Loach should put up his hands. The Sten-guns never wavered.

Loach half-raised his hands. The Sten-guns never wavered. The sergeant expertly ran his hands over Loach.

'Right, sir,' said the sergeant. 'I think we'd better take you back now.'

'I'm not coming,' said Loach.

'This way, sir,' said the sergeant.

'No,' said Loach.

'Please, sir,' said the sergeant. But he wasn't pleading, only reasoning with a stubborn child. 'You know the regulations.'

'No,' said Loach again, and turned to run.

That was when something hit him, and all was darkness.

57

It wasn't a cell but it was bare, and there were unmistakable bars on the window. Loach lay on the bed fully dressed. His head hurt like hell.

'What were you trying to do?' asked Shaw. He was sitting on a chair next to the wooden table.

'What do you think?' said Loach. The effort caused a sharp pain, and he groaned.

'I'm sorry about that,' said Shaw, without sympathy. 'But it was a bloody stupid thing to try and run away. They could have shot you.'

'And now you're going to court-martial me,' said Loach.

'We could,' said Shaw.

'I'd like that,' said Loach. 'I'd like that very much. I'd like to start quoting some King's Regulations.'

'Quote them all you want, Captain Loach,' said Shaw. 'All day long if you like.'

Loach made the effort, and sat up on one elbow.

'You can't get away with this,' he said. 'Sir.'

'I think you're still suffering from that knock on the head,' said Shaw.

'I want to see my commanding officer,' said Loach.

'I am your commanding officer,' said Shaw.

'No. My CO. Of my Section.'

Hell, his head hurt.

'You are under my command,' said Shaw. 'For special training. Of course, after last night's little escapade, charges may be brought.'

'I'm under arrest?'

'No,' said Shaw. 'You are, shall we say, confined to quarters.'

'These are not my quarters,' said Loach.

'You need treatment, for that bump,' said Shaw. 'It's easier to look after you here.'

'One day,' said Loach, 'somebody is going to get away from here.'

'Well,' said Shaw, standing up, 'you're obviously a bit under the weather. I'll see you later.'

'Damn you,' said Loach.

Shaw stopped.

'We are very informal here, and we don't stand on protocol,' he said. 'But I am your superior officer, and I think you should remember it.'

'You can make that another charge,' said Loach.

Shaw sat down again. Suddenly, he changed his approach.

'Look,' he said, 'I know it's difficult for you. It is for everybody here. But don't you realize you are all here for your own protection. Once you are compromised, it wouldn't be safe to use you. The only reason we run this place is to have somewhere to hide you away until it's all right to use you.'

'You've put me away because of that girl,' said Loach. 'Everybody in here has done something you're afraid of . . .'

Shaw shook his head.

'Ask yourself something, Loach,' he said.

Loach said nothing.

'Ask yourself what you know.'

Loach's mouth was dry.

'What are you talking about?' he said.

'You know the place,' said Shaw. 'You know the information Raoul Dubois was bringing over to Jester. The information you were bringing. The place.'

'You know I can't talk about that,' said Loach.

'And you know we can't take the risk that you might.'

'Damn it,' said Loach. 'I don't have to prove my loyalty. I don't have to prove any bloody thing. So I know the place. What does that prove?'

'You're vulnerable, that's all,' said Shaw. 'The little incident in London made them realize how vulnerable. Soon it won't matter. Then you'll be back in things.'

He smiled reassuringly.

'Soon?' said Loach, bitterly.

'When they've landed. When it doesn't matter who knows the place. Soon.'

Shaw got up once more.

At the door, he turned.

'We're not going to keep you in a dungeon, you know. You can carry on as normal. I might just ask you to keep within five hundred yards of the house,' he said.

'And if I don't?' said Loach.

Shaw just smiled. Then he knocked on the inside of the door. Loach heard a key turn, and the door was opened. Loach saw an Army sergeant outside the door.

The man was armed.

And when the door was slammed behind Shaw, the key was turned again.

God, his head hurt.

Martin surfaced in the Cooler the way they all had done. He suddenly arrived, and was part of the community. Since nobody asked many questions, he was accepted as one of them. Another inmate who, because of an indiscretion or a failure or a weakness, could no longer be relied on – and would now have to spend his time on ice in Inverloch.

Clare was playing table tennis in the games room when Martin came in. It was the first time she had seen him in this place.

'Hallo,' he said.

She had finished the game, and her partner, a taciturn Irishman, had nodded and wandered off. All she knew about the man, from something he had let slip, was that he was an explosives expert. How he came to be inside they didn't discuss. But he played good table tennis.

Martin strolled over.

'Have another game?' he said.

'No,' said Clare.

He put the bat down.

'Well,' he said, 'and how are you?'

'Do you really want to know?' she said. Her tone said enough.

'I suppose I shouldn't ask,' said Martin. 'Tell me, what's it like here?'

'Every home comfort,' said Clare, and turned away. But he was obviously not going to be shrugged off.

'I imagine I'll get used to it,' said Martin. 'Everybody else seems to have.'

He looked at the two men playing their feverish match on the other table. They were completely caught up in the fury of their exchanges.

'Let's go and have a coffee,' said Martin.

Clare shrugged. 'All right,' she said. She seemed to have resigned herself to his company.

In the lounge he raised his coffee cup to her like a toast.

'At least it's nice to find you here,' he said.

'Really?' said Clare. She sounded bored.

'I didn't actually know what to expect,' said Martin. 'No clue at all.'

'What are you supposed to be doing here?' she asked, but with complete disinterest.

'I'm on a special training course,' said Martin. 'I was quite surprised, actually. The orders came at two hours' notice. It's all very hush-hush.'

'Yes, it is,' said Clare.

'Colonel Shaw hasn't told me very much,' said Martin. 'You've met him, haven't you?'

'We all have,' she said.

She finished her coffee.

'Tell me,' he said, 'what on earth do people do here off duty. On Saturday nights? Where do they go?'

'They don't,' said Clare.

He appeared really surprised.

'You mean we're stuck here?'

'Yes,' said Clare.

'The whole time?'

'The whole time,' said Clare.

He made a point of appearing to digest this. Then:

'What about you?' he asked. 'Have you finished your training?'

'You'd better ask Colonel Shaw,' said Clare.

Then, quite casually, she asked him:

'This training course of yours. Did they tell you why?'

'What do you mean?'

She tried to find the right words.

'Did they send you here because . . .'

She stopped.

'Yes?' said Martin, quite innocent.

'I mean, had there been any sort of trouble . . . did you . . .'

Again, she faltered.

'I don't quite understand,' said Martin. 'What sort of trouble?'

'Sometimes,' said Clare, 'people get sent here because they have become a problem.'

'Oh really?' said Martin. Then, as if meaning had suddenly become clear to him:

'Are you saying this place is some kind of punishment?'

She smiled.

'Why, have you noticed anything strange about anybody?' he asked.

'Look around,' said Clare.

'You're imagining things,' he said firmly.

'I think I'll go for a walk,' she said, and stood up.

'I'll come with you,' he said eagerly.

'Some other time,' said Clare sweetly.

'All right,' he said, a shade disappointed. Then he called after her: 'Oh, Clare, I don't suppose you've heard from your father lately?'

'No,' said Clare. 'I haven't.'

As she walked out, his eyes did not let go of her.

59

Loach reappeared in the community, sitting in the library in his favourite armchair, eating in the dining-room, and keeping to himself. He looked a little drawn, like a man who's had a tough experience.

Clare was surprised that he made no attempt to corner her. Before he suddenly disappeared, he usually descended on her as soon as she was around. Now he seemed to prefer his own company.

The second evening he was once more around, Clare sat down in the armchair next to him.

'What happened to you?' she asked.

'Nothing,' said Loach.

'When you weren't around, I thought you'd really given it a try,' said Clare, brightly.

'I don't know what you're talking about,' he grunted.

'Oh, all right then,' said Clare, and got up.

'No,' he said. He put his hand gently on her arm. 'Stay. I'm sorry.'

'I only wondered where you were,' she said. 'God knows there aren't many places to go to here.'

'I never went anywhere,' said Loach. 'But I got a bump on the head.'

'From what?'

'Being too curious,' said Loach. 'It just doesn't pay.'

Clare was instantly interested.

'Do talk sense,' she said impatiently.

'All right, I'll tell you,' he said. 'I took a little stroll. Maybe I wasn't going to come back. But they found me. And the bastards aren't very gentle.'

'How far did you get?' asked Clare.

'A few miles,' said Loach.

Martin came into the library. He spotted them and walked over.

'May I join you?' he asked pleasantly. He pulled up another armchair, and smiled inquiringly, looking at Loach.

'Jim is a friend of mine,' said Clare, and Loach nodded coldly. 'And this is Martin.'

'Who's Martin?' said Loach. He was surly.

'Martin and I keep bumping into each other,' said Clare. 'Don't we, Martin?'

'Oh?' said Loach. 'Where?'

'You'd never guess,' said Clare. 'The training place. And the Savoy. Now here.'

'You get around,' said Loach, unfriendly.

'It's a small war,' said Martin.

'What were you doing at the Savoy?' asked Loach.

'I was having dinner, and there was Martin with some glamorous WREN,' said Clare. 'What does she do, Martin?'

'She comforts the troops,' said Martin.

'Maybe she should do some comforting around here,' snapped Loach.

'Absolutely,' said Martin.

Loach looked at his watch.

'It's getting late for me,' he said. 'If you'll excuse me.'

'You're quite right,' said Clare. 'I'm off too.'

They left Martin with polite nods.

Clare was undressing, and had unfastened her stockings when there was a tap at the door.

'Who's that?' she called out.

'I have to see you,' said a voice. It was Loach.

'I'm just going to bed,' she said. 'I'll see you in the morning.'

'I'll only be a minute,' he said urgently, trying to keep his voice low. 'I have to talk to you.'

'Not now,' she said.

'Please,' said Loach. 'It's important.'

Something was wrong. Hastily she pulled a wrap round her, and unlocked the door. She opened it a little.

'I'm tired,' she said. 'You can't come in.'

She tried to shut the door, but he held it.

'I'm not bloody well going to rape you,' he snarled. 'It's important I tell you.'

She wanted to know more.

'All right,' she said, clutching the wrap tighter.

He came in and sat down on the bed.

'Clare,' he said. 'That man. Tonight. What do you know about him?'

'Martin?'

'What's his job?' said Loach.

His eyes took her figure in. The wrap did not conceal the swell of her breasts. He felt excitement. No, he tried to tell himself. Not now. Not her.

'I don't know,' said Clare. Despite herself, she was flushing. His eyes betrayed his mind. She wanted him out of the room quickly – but she also wanted to find out more.

'Why are you so interested?' she asked.

He felt the craving to hurt her. To reach out, and make her cry in anguish. That feverish compulsion to make them scream with pain started to grow. He clenched his hands. He must not betray himself.

'He's asking a lot of questions,' he said.

'Oh?'

Sitting in the chair, she was glad there was a little distance between them.

'The Dutchman,' said Loach. 'He's been asking him things. And that Navy chap. And he's too bloody curious about everything. He hangs about everybody. He's always chatting to people.'

'Is that a crime?' asked Clare. She pulled the wrap close over her thighs.

'Here?' said Loach, and left the question unanswered. She had a good body, damn it. Nice legs. She was strong . . .

If he stayed, it was dangerous.

'He's after something,' said Loach. 'He's a snooper. Maybe we should tell somebody.'

He got up.

'I thought you might know about him,' he said.

'Why should I?' asked Clare. Thank God, the man was going.

Loach smiled. His eyes were very bright.

'Good night,' he said.

And he closed the door behind him softly.

Clare sat in the chair motionless.

Her heart was beating, very fast.

60

Grau's masters on the other side seemed to suspect nothing. They acknowledged the doctored messages he sent, and they periodically gave him instructions to follow up this or check on that as they had always done.

When Grau transmitted, one of Deception's men would watch every movement of his key finger, and they recorded each burst of Morse and monitored the relay, checking and cross-checking that nothing unusual had happened.

Oscar was being a very good boy indeed, and Deception seemed satisfied.

'I do like turning 'em,' he said to Ince with professional pride. 'There's something very satisfying making their people send our stuff to them.'

'It cuts both ways,' said Ince, a little maliciously. He could not resist pricking Deception's conceit. 'Remember the Dutch débâcle? They did it to us.'

'Hardly my department,' said Deception. 'If operators in the field omit the bluff check, and nobody takes any notice this end, you could hardly blame my side of it.'

'What about Oscar's bluff check?' said Ince.

'He swears his circuit works differently,' said Deception. 'And signals haven't noticed anything unusual, one way or the other.'

'Maybe that's his check,' said Ince.

Deception looked at him pityingly.

'Don't you think we've compared his old transmission pattern with the one he's doing for us?' he said, patiently.

'And?'

'The pattern's identical.'

He poured himself some of Ince's illegally acquired PX whisky.

'How are your problems? Found the phantom of Inverloch?'

'No,' said Ince. 'There's been nothing more. Having alerted his people, he's now off the air.'

Deception put the bottle back.

'I think he'll only send one more message,' he said cheerfully. 'When he's got what he's there for. He won't care after that. But that's the one message that matters. And you'd better stop it ever going out.'

'Thank you,' said Ince coldly.

'Has your man found out anything?' said Deception casually. 'About your suspects?'

'He hasn't found the radio. He's been asking a lot of questions and getting very few answers. They don't talk much in the Cooler.'

'You should be grateful,' said Deception. 'At least they're well trained.'

The phone rang, and Ince took it. He handed the receiver to Deception.

'For you,' he said. Deception made himself very free and easy with other people's whisky, and other people's phone extensions, he thought. He hadn't even told him he was expecting a call.

Deception listened, made approving noises, and then hung up.

'Just a bulletin on Oscar,' he said. 'I like to be kept informed.'

'How is he?' said Ince, who hadn't seen Grau for a day or two.

'Asking if we can supply a woman,' said Deception.

'Cocky bastard,' said Ince.

'If he's really good to me, I'll get him one,' said Deception.

'And if he isn't?'

'I'll hang him,' said Deception. 'Cheers.'

He walked over to the map on the wall.

'You must have enough people in the Cooler to start the second front,' he said.

'Hardly,' said Ince. Sometimes he lacked any sense of humour. Especially on this subject.

'How many? Twenty? Thirty? Forty?'

'Enough,' said Ince. Almost as if he wanted to justify himself, he added: 'What else can we do with them?'

'My dear chap,' said Deception, 'I'm not criticizing. I just hope it never blows up on you.'

'So do I,' said Ince.

'Anyway, there's one marvellous thing about it,' said Deception.

'Oh?' said Ince cautiously. You never knew with this man.

'It must be driving our German friends scatty, biting their nails about Inverloch and the inmates.'

'They know, you think?' said Ince. He was a little anxious now.

'Of course they do,' said Deception.

'How?'

'Oscar told them, who else?' said Deception.

And he smiled.

'How do you know?' said Ince, shaken.

'I instructed him to do it,' said Deception.

'You what?'

'They were on to it anyway,' said Deception. 'It was only right that they should get confirmation from their own man.'

'You must be mad,' said Ince.

'I just enjoy breaking rules,' said Deception. 'It's fun.'

'Whose game are you playing anyway,' said Ince. He was ratty.

Deception wasn't offended at all.

'You know,' he said, 'sometimes I get to wondering myself.'

61

Martin's body was found the next day, behind one of the outbuildings near the big house. He had been garrotted, and the thin piano wire his killer had twisted round his neck had bitten deep into thc flesh, and almost severed the windpipe.

It was an ugly death, and expertly done.

Martin was fully clothed when they found him, at first light, and he must have been prowling around the big mansion when his murderer crept up from behind, and tightened the garrotte.

Near his body lay a torch, which he had apparently dropped.

The way he had been killed was the classic example of the stealthy assassination in the dark, such as one used against the German sentries.

The method most of those in the Cooler had been specially taught.

There was only one passenger in the Lysander that landed in the grounds. The little plane taxied to a halt on the lawn, as it so often did on courier trips in the fields of France and Holland, and the passenger jumped out.

Major Craddock was an SIB specialist, and they could tell him a lot more than they dared with an ordinary investigator. He was also adept at producing the kind of report on paper that they needed. The truth he would tell them verbally.

At Scotland Yard, he had been a Murder Squad superintendent who kept in the background, and whose services the War Office urgently requested in 1940.

Since then, Craddock had vanished from sight, and nobody had really become aware of the fact.

'What will be your official explanation about this business?' Craddock asked Shaw.

'A training accident,' said Shaw.

'Really?' said Craddock.

'Night training,' said Shaw.

'Do you have night training here?' asked Craddock.

Shaw looked him straight in the eye.

'We have every kind of training,' he said.

Craddock nodded. He approved.

'Of course, I know what the man was here for,' he said.

'Oh, do you?' said Shaw. 'What was that?'

Again Craddock was pleased. A man after his own heart.

He opened his briefcase, and took out a sheet of paper.

'I'd like to ask these people a few questions, Colonel,' he said.

Shaw looked at the names.

'Certainly,' he said. 'Just these?'

'Just those,' said Craddock.

He hesitated a moment. Then he said: 'He was looking for something when he was killed. Did he give you any hint?'

'Good Lord, no,' said Shaw. 'It was much better that I shouldn't know. You understand?'

Craddock understood fully. This man really spoke his language.

'You haven't told anybody about it, have you?' he asked. 'I mean, the civilian police, for instance?'

'It's entirely a military matter, surely,' said Shaw. 'They don't investigate battle-course accidents at OCTUs, do they?'

'Of course not,' said Craddock, 'nothing to do with them.'

'Perhaps there'll have to be a board ...'

'I leave that tc London, Colonel,' said Craddock.

He pulled another sheet of paper out of his briefcase.

'Now, let's see, footprints negative,' he said, and looked up at Shaw for confirmation.

Shaw nodded.

'Fingerprints, negative of course. Hardly be any point to look on piano wire,' said Craddock. 'Method of garrotting. Ah, yes.'

He underlined something with his pencil.

'They're doing a post-mortem, of course,' he said, 'but I don't think it'll tell us anything, except that the murderer has been excellently trained, and is a credit to us all.'

He put all the papers back in the briefcase.

'You know, Colonel,' he said, 'sometimes I wonder what will happen when we release all your charges into civvy street.'

He looked at his watch.

'If you don't mind, I think I ought to get started,' he said.

'Of course,' said Shaw. 'I'll lay on the facilities.'

'I want to rattle 'em a bit,' said Craddock. 'I don't suppose it will work, but if we find your killer we find your mysterious radio operator.'

'You know about that?' said Shaw, slightly surprised.

'Oh, I heard something about it,' said Craddock vaguely.

63

'You've seen the list?' the colonel asked Ince, showing him the telex.

'Yes, sir,' said Ince. He wished the colonel would let him go back to his office. Things were moving too fast.

The colonel looked at it again.

'I see SIB wants some information from the Dutch Section,' he said. 'Apparently there's a Dutchman in Inverloch they're quite interested in.'

'I saw that,' said Ince.

'You know him?'

'Only that Martin was rather interested in him too,' said Ince.

'Oh really? Perhaps he's our man,' said the colonel hopefully.

'Perhaps,' said Ince.

'Had Martin got anywhere?' The colonel desperately wanted reassuring.

'I think our Trojan Horse was getting worried,' said Ince. 'That was something.'

'I suppose so,' said the colonel. 'Poor devil.'

Ince raised his eyebrows.

'I mean Martin,' said the colonel. 'It's these bureaucrats who make me spew. Martin cannot be listed as killed in action. Murdered hunting a bloody traitor, and all he is is killed on active service.'

'Does it matter?' said Ince, who was neither god-fearing nor sentimental.

'It does to the family,' said the colonel stiffly.

'Dead is dead, sir,' said Ince.

The colonel decided that he was right all along, he had never wanted to play golf with Ince.

So he changed the subject.

'This Deception business,' he said.

'Yes?' said Ince, warily.

'Is it really working. Using this Oscar?'

'I'm only on the sidelines, sir,' said Ince.

'It's your operation. You're right in it,' said the colonel.

'It's not an operation,' said Ince. 'It's a game.'

'Well, I hope you don't lose it,' said the colonel frostily.

Ince did not say a word. He knew when it was pointless.

'I have never been keen on this idea of turning enemy agents,' said the colonel, as a parting shot. 'I wonder how you can all be so sure they haven't turned you.'

64

When Clare's turn came, she was shown into an office on the administrative corridor of the mansion. She had not been in this part before. The staircase that led to it had a silken cord across it, and the inmates never used it.

What she did notice as an RAF sergeant, one of the staff NCOs, led her along it was that, unlike other military offices, there were no name tags or departmental signs on the doors. Just large roman numbers. The sergeant stopped at No IX.

'Here you are, miss,' he said, and knocked.

'Enter,' said a voice, and Clare went in, not knowing quite what to expect. The bald man had merely told her to keep herself available, and she'd be told what they needed her for. The waiting had made her nervous.

And also very curious, because she had no idea what the Lysander had brought. It was the first time she had seen a plane land in the grounds. Her first thought was that they were bringing in a new resident, so important, so secret loaded that he had to be rushed into his captivity at the highest speed. No travel vouchers, or train journeys to Inverloch for him.

But she never caught a glimpse of the lone passenger, and now she wasn't so sure anyway.

Craddock stood up, and indicated a chair in front of the desk he was occupying. To Clare's surprise, a shorthand writer was sitting in a corner.

'Thank you for coming, Miss Gilbert,' said Craddock, as if she had had any choice. 'I'm Major Craddock.'

Clare sat down, and watched him without making it too obvious, she hoped.

'I don't know if you've been told,' said Craddock, 'but there's been an unfortunate accident. I believe you knew the young officer.'

And he pushed over Martin's photograph.

'Accident?' repeated Clare, staring at the picture.

'I'm afraid he's dead,' said Craddock, 'and I'm just compiling a report. So I have to talk to people who knew him. It's very sad.'

'I hardly knew ... Martin,' said Clare.

'Oh?' Craddock made much of his astonishment. 'I must have been given the wrong information. I understood he trained with you.'

'No,' said Clare. 'I once met him. At Ferny Bank. He wasn't training with me.'

'But you saw him more often than that, surely?'

'Well,' said Clare. 'Not really. In London once.'

'Where?'

'At the Savoy.'

Craddock was pleased. 'You had dinner with him?'

'No,' said Clare. 'We happened to bump into each other. He was out with somebody else, having dinner too.'

'I see.'

Craddock studied her, making it very obvious.

'I tell you what I'd like to do, Miss Gilbert,' he said. 'You tell us all you know about him. We take it down in shorthand, and I'll have it typed, and then you can sign it and everything's nice and tidy.'

'I don't understand,' said Clare.

'I'd like you to make a statement,' said Craddock. He saw her frozen face. 'You must bear with me. I've been a policeman all my life, and I'm lost without statements. They're my bread and butter.'

'But I can't tell you anything about Martin,' said Clare.

'Then it'll be a very short statement,' said Craddock reasonably.

He turned to the shorthand writer. He looked at his watch.

'1435 hours. The date. Statement of Clare Gilbert. Ready?'

The pencil flew across the pad. The shorthand writer nodded.

'Shall I start it off for you,' said Craddock. ' "I knew the dead man. We had been assigned to the same training unit, and we became acquainted. Later, I met him socially in a London hotel and—" '

'That isn't right,' said Clare. 'I didn't meet him socially at any hotel.'

'Well, it wasn't a business meeting, was it?' said Craddock.

'I was having dinner with my father, and Martin came over for a few seconds,' she said.

'Ah,' said Craddock. 'I see.'

'Why do I have to make this statement?' said Clare.

'Not just you,' said Craddock reassuringly. 'It's a pure formality. I'm talking to everybody who met him.'

'But it's an accident, you said.'

'My trouble is I can't leave well alone,' said Craddock.

'How did he die?' asked Clare. 'What actually happened?'

Craddock didn't seem to have heard her.

'Tell me,' he said, 'did you have any idea what Martin was doing here?'

'What are any of us doing here, Major Craddock?' said Clare.

'Did you think he was here on any kind of special duty?' He said it very gently.

'Special—' Clare said. 'What special duty?'

'You thought he was just like everybody else?'

'I thought he had been sent to this place because ...' she began.

'Yes?'

'Maybe he'd been compromised.' There, she thought. I can use that nice phrase too.

'Is that what people are here, compromised?' asked Craddock.

'I thought you would know,' said Clare. 'They don't tell us much.'

'Didn't you think Martin was asking a lot of questions?' said Craddock.

'Maybe he was,' said Clare. 'What are you trying to say?'

'I was asking you,' said Craddock politely.

'Was – was there something special about Martin, then?' asked Clare. 'His job, I mean?'

'Miss Gilbert, you're almost asking as many questions as me,' said Craddock genially. 'But I'm the one who's supposed to ask you things.'

'Sorry,' said Clare.

'Before the – accident. Did you talk to Martin?'

'Just for a few seconds, in the lounge. We were having coffee.'

'You do make it sound like a seaside hotel,' said Craddock. 'Just a few seconds? Your meetings with Martin all seem to have been very brief.'

Clare was concentrating.

'Wait,' she said. 'I remember he said something why he was here. He said – yes, he said he was on a "special training course".'

'And then?'

'I was very tired,' said Clare.

'Of course,' said Craddock. 'All this country air.'

'You see, I really can't help you much,' said Clare.

'I think we can all summarize it neatly in a short statement,' said Craddock. 'I'll have it ready for you to sign.'

'Is that all?' said Clare.

'Only one small point I forgot,' said Craddock. 'The night the – accident happened. The suggestion is that Martin met his – er – death about 4 or 5 AM. Goodness knows how doctors get so accurate.'

'Yes,' said Clare. She wondered what was coming.

'My problem is that I like to tidy everything up,' said Craddock. 'Unfortunately, it's really impossible in a place like this. I mean, nobody can account for their movements, can they? They were all asleep.'

'Why should they?' said Clare. 'Why do you need to know where they were?'

'But just suppose somebody had been up at that time?' said Craddock. 'It would be so useful to know.'

'I wasn't,' said Clare.

'Of course not,' said Craddock. 'You were asleep in your room. So was everybody else. It's a good thing we don't need an alibi, isn't it?'

'You're trying to say something,' whispered Clare.

'I'm only talking off the top of my head, Miss Gilbert,' said Craddock. 'Bear with me. I'm so glad you're not involved. Because, supposing I wanted proof that you were where you said you were, I could never have it.'

This bastard was accusing her of something. She knew it. He was trying to say, Martin was murdered, and he was killed in a way you've been trained to kill, and I suspect something and I want to break your nerve.

Clare had courage.

'As a matter of fact, you're wrong, Major Craddock,' she said. 'If I needed it, I do have an alibi.'

'Really?' said Craddock.

Clare glanced at the shorthand writer.

'Does this have to be taken down?' she asked.

He was terribly understanding. 'Oh, I see. You want this to be between the two of us?'

She nodded.

'I'll call you,' he said to the shorthand writer, who quietly got up and left the room.

'Now, my dear,' said Craddock, 'you've volunteered all this. You do understand that.'

'You want to know where I was between 4 and 5 AM when Martin – died.'

'You don't have to give me an alibi,' said Craddock. 'You're not accused of anything.'

'But you don't just want to take my word.' She said it bitterly.

'I'm a policeman,' said Craddock. 'Proof is my religion.'

'I was with somebody,' said Clare, flushed. 'Not only between 4 and 5. All night.'

'Yes,' said Craddock gently.

'I was with a man,' said Clare defiantly. 'It is possible here, you know.'

Craddock nodded. 'But you won't tell me his name?' he said, still very gently.

'You want an alibi, don't you,' said Clare, tightly. 'All right. You can have one. I was sleeping with a Captain Loach.'

65

After tea, Loach was brought to Room IX, and Craddock introduced himself as an officer of the Special Investigation Branch.

'I'm making some routine inquiries,' he said.

'So I've heard,' said Loach.

'Who told you?' asked Craddock mildly.

'Gossip flies around here,' said Loach. 'And rumour. We have little else to feed us.'

'You resent being here?' asked Craddock.

'I should now be on a key mission,' said Loach. 'Not sitting here on my arse.'

'But you're here—?' said Craddock.

'Yes, for "special training",' said Loach. 'The phrase must be coming out of your ears.'

Craddock nodded to the shorthand writer.

'1710 hours. Today's date. Statement of Captain James Loach. That's it.'

He looked at Loach.

'You know an officer was found dead in the grounds,' he began.

'And you want to know who murdered him,' said Loach.

'I don't think I used the word murder,' said Craddock.

'Look,' said Loach. 'I'll help you if I can. I'll do what I can. But don't treat me like a moron. You wouldn't be here if he hadn't been murdered. You wouldn't be asking these questions. All right?'

There was a pause. The shorthand writer waited expectantly. He did not look at either of them, but stared vacantly into space, pencil poised.

'You were transferred here after a little problem in London, I believe,' said Craddock.

'They made it a problem,' said Loach.

'Very unfortunate,' said Craddock.

Loach waited for it. Did you know who Martin was? How did you get on with him? When did you last see him? Did you guess what he was doing here?

Instead, Craddock asked:

'How well do you know Miss Gilbert?'

This Loach hadn't expected.

'I know her,' he said.

'Wasn't she in your Section?' said Craddock.

'Yes,' said Loach. 'Same command. But one compartment doesn't have much to do with the other. We share mutual amenities like Major Ince.'

'Anyway,' said Craddock, 'you didn't by any chance go for a walk on the night Martin died?'

'You mean, did I bump into him in a dark corner, and kill him, no,' said Loach.

'But where were you?' pressed Craddock.

'There's no point in telling you,' said Loach.

'Why not?'

'Because I can't prove it.'

'Shouldn't you leave that to me?' said Craddock.

'All right,' said Loach. 'I was in bed.'

Craddock nodded. 'That's all right,' he said.

'But how can I prove it?'

'I think you can,' said Craddock.

'How?' repeated Loach.

'Because I already know who you slept with,' said Craddock, watching him intently.

'I'm not saying anything,' said Loach.

'It's in your interest,' said Craddock.

Loach licked his dry lips.

'No,' he said. 'There's nothing I can say.'

'You see,' said Craddock, 'I have a signed statement. It does you credit to play Sir Galahad, but I assure you you are off the hook.'

'What signed statement?' said Loach.

'The girl you slept with.'

'Then you don't need mine,' said Loach.

'I do like to tidy things up,' said Craddock. 'Your reluctance confirms her statement anyway. But I'd love it in writing from you.'

'Exactly what do you want me to say?' asked Loach.

Craddock turned to the shorthand writer.

'Would you read back my first question about Miss Gilbert?' he requested.

The shorthand writer looked for the line.

'"How well do you know Miss Gilbert?"' he read out in a monotone.

'You haven't answered me yet, Captain Loach,' said Craddock reproachfully.

'I said I know her,' said Loach curtly.

'How well?'

'I don't see that my relationship with Miss Gilbert is of importance to you, your inquiry, or anybody else,' said Loach.

'I'm not interested in prying into private relationships,' said Craddock. 'But this is important.'

'I don't want to talk about it,' said Loach.

'There is a relationship though ...' Craddock waited.

'She's an attractive girl,' said Loach.

'Yes,' said Craddock. 'Indeed.'

He looked at Loach with interest. Loach stared back at him.

'You like going for long walks, I believe,' said Craddock.

'I did,' said Loach. 'I took a very long one, and after that they discouraged me.'

'Really?'

Loach turned on him with distaste. 'It was the Cooler's equivalent of falling down the stairs at the police station.'

'Oh, dear,' said Craddock, 'you had an accident.'

'Yes,' snarled Loach. 'You can call it that.'

'And you spent the night in question in the company of Miss Clare Gilbert.'

Loach thought.

Then he said:

'All right. I'll give you your statement.'

66

Deception was in high good humour.

'Look at this,' he said. 'A shopping list for Oscar. It's their latest "most urgent" for him. They know it's now or never.'

'CONFIRM HIGHEST PRIORITY THAT PAS DE CALAIS DESIGNATED LANDING AREA AND BATTLE ORDER CONCENTRATED ON SOUTH EAST ENGLAND SUBSTANTIATES WEIGHT OF LANDINGS TO BE IN CALAIS AND DUNKIRK AREAS ALSO OBTAIN IF POSSIBLE CODENAMES FOR SELECTED LANDING SPOTS AS THIS INVALUABLE IN CONFIRMING OVERALL PLAN PLEASE GIVE THIS UTMOST PRIORITY EVEN IF NORMALLY UNWARRANTED RISK INVOLVED' read the intercept.

'Interesting,' said Ince.

'Interesting,' said Deception. 'That's putting it mildly. ' "Give utmost priority even if normally unwarranted risk involved" ! You know what they're telling him. You're expendable. We don't mind if they catch you after this, but do this one last thing for us because it's vital. I think Oscar will be quite hurt.'

'What have you done about it?' asked Ince.

'Just acknowledged it, of course,' said Deception. 'Oscar doesn't have to lose any sleep over it, lucky bastard. It's the lads and I who have to come up with a real little masterpiece.'

'I'm sure you will,' said Ince drily.

Deception put the paper in the safe.

'You annoy me sometimes, Ince,' he said. 'You're just as tricky a customer as any of us, and you know you'd sell your grandmother to put one over.'

'My grandmother's dead,' said Ince, without humour.

'The point is,' said Deception, 'that we've been working very hard to sell them the idea that the Pas de Calais is the objective of Overlord. If we can keep it up, they may actually fall for it. I think Oscar will be very useful. However, if ...'

He stopped.

'If they find out the real story,' said Ince. He didn't finish.

Deception nodded.

'And the one place they can find it out could be where there is somebody who knows Overlord,' he said. 'Somebody who is a problem anyway ...'

'I'm sorry,' said Ince. 'I wish I had some news. SIB's stirring things up in the Cooler, but we haven't got anywhere so far.'

'No further radio traffic?'

'Silent as the proverbial grave,' said Ince. 'Twenty-four hours' surveillance, but nothing. That transmitter is keeping quiet. He probably suspects we might be on to him, and will only risk one message.'

'That's *the* message,' said Deception.

'Exactly.'

'I'd like to get drunk tonight,' said Deception. 'Have you got any of that lovely PX whisky left?'

'You'll have to come to my place,' said Ince.

'Let's enjoy it while we can,' said Deception.

As he locked up, he asked:

'Do you cheat on your wife, Ince?'

'I'm not married,' said Ince, who wasn't, at the moment. 'Do you?'

'Ah,' said Deception.

They went down in the lift. They were quite alone in it, and it was safe to ask the question.

'You realize what tomorrow is, don't you?' said Deception.

Ince frowned.

'What?'

'Minus twenty-nine. Twenty-nine days to go.'

It hit Ince. 'God, you're right,' he said.

'So it's too late to change anything even if we wanted to,' said Deception.

The lift arrived at ground level, and they immediately changed the subject.

But it took Ince a long time to get even slightly merry that night.

In fact, when he made the usual check call to the duty officer at midnight, he sounded dead sober.

Two hours later, Deception took a cab home and spent the rest of the night sitting in an armchair, with a pencil and big notepad. From time to time he wrote a few lines, read them, changed his mind, crossed something out here and altered something there.

He worked very hard.

He was composing the priority message that Oscar was going to send from the bookshop within a few hours.

67

'Why did you do it?' asked Loach.

They were standing on the banks of the loch, their backs to the great house. It was a beautiful May evening, and ahead of them stretched the grey blue waters, and in the distance the Scottish hills.

'I thought you were in trouble,' said Clare.

'Why?' said Loach.

She looked very pretty, with the wind blowing a strand of hair across her forehead.

'It was the way he talked. The questions he asked.'

'I don't really need an alibi, you know,' said Loach gently.

'Don't you?' said Clare. Her head turned and she looked at him with great wondering eyes.

'You don't really think I – I killed him, do you?'

He didn't seem particularly put out at the suggestion, more intrigued that she should think it.

'I don't know,' said Clare, studying the waters of the loch.

'For what reason?' he asked.

'How do I know,' said Clare. She pushed the errant hairs out of her eyes. 'You seemed very interested in him. Too interested, maybe.'

'Isn't that what they've taught us – anybody who asks too many questions is dangerous,' said Loach. 'I was curious, that's all.'

'So was he,' said Clare.

They slowly started to stroll.

'Anyway, that's not the reason you tried to cover up for me,' said Loach.

Clare did not reply.

'Why should you care if I'm in a mess?' asked Loach. He stopped, and faced her.

'What does it matter to you?' he said.

She turned away.

'Well?' he said.

'Maybe I don't want to see you dragged away,' she said in a low voice.

'Oh, come on,' he said.

'Leave me alone,' said Clare, and walked off at a fast pace.

He caught up with her, grabbed her arm.

'No,' he said, 'that isn't good enough.'

'All right,' she said, and her voice sounded bitter. 'It isn't good enough. May I go now?'

Loach continued to walk at her side.

'You know when I came to your room the night . . .'

She nodded.

'I wanted to stay.'

She nodded.

'You know why I didn't?' He laughed without joy. 'Because I could see how you looked at me. Terrified. Shaking that I might grab you. And the relief on your face when I left. I haven't forgotten that.'

She said nothing.

'So why did you tell that lie?' he said harshly.

She swallowed. 'Maybe you're wrong,' she said.

'I'm not wrong about that,' he said. 'You were afraid of me. You didn't want me to sleep with you. All you wanted was to be rid of me.'

'Can't you guess why?' said Clare.

'If somebody spits you out, you don't really care a damn why you taste bad to them,' said Loach unpleasantly.

'I was afraid,' she said. 'I am afraid.'

'Of what?'

'You,' she said, and walked on rapidly.

'Hey,' he said, 'why afraid?'

'You know yourself,' she said. 'What happens to you.'

His eyes narrowed.

'Go on.'

'Nothing. I – I don't want it to happen to me.'

'What are you talking about?' said Loach. But he knew quite well.

'Isn't that why you are here?' she flung at him. 'After what you did to that girl? Isn't it that if you go with a woman, something happens to you . . .'

'What girl?' asked Loach quietly.

'Playtime is over,' said Clare.

'No, please,' he said. He could be very nice. 'No, not like this.'

'I just thought I could help you,' she said, and Loach thought he saw something in her eyes. No, not a tear, surely? 'That was something I could do. It would clear you. It . . .'

She stopped. Then, she was in control again.

'I'm sorry if I've embarrassed you, Captain Loach,' she said. 'The last thing I wanted was to compromise you.' She smiled thinly. 'Nice word, isn't it, compromise?'

'Clare . . .' he said.

She walked on, towards the house.

'Clare,' he said again, and took her arm.

'Let's go to my room,' he said softly.

She did not react. But neither did she shake off the arm that was beginning to guide her very firmly.

68

They got very drunk. Loach had managed to acquire a bottle of brandy, and they went to his room, and forgot the time.

Craddock saw them going up the staircase together. Anyone watching him would hardly have realized that he was interested, but soon afterwards he went to Shaw's office and made a call on the scrambler line to London.

Despite the alcohol, Clare was keeping some channel of her mind alert. She did not flinch when Loach put his arm round her, but as he fumbled with her bra she looked, like a detached observer on the side-line, for some tell-tale sign that she was in danger.

It didn't seem to come. Yet.

They lay on the bed, and it was the first time that Clare had been with a man since that night in the Praed Street hotel. It was Loach's body she felt, but it was Tony she saw in the shadows above her.

She had switched off Tony's memory because she felt guilty. Guilty about failing him in what he wanted. If he hadn't got killed, it wouldn't have mattered. No pressures, they had agreed. Just fun. But that last night it had gone wrong, and he never had the chance to touch another woman, and she was sorry. She would have liked to have given him a good send-off.

'It isn't so bad, is it?' whispered Loach, nuzzling her.

'No, darling,' said Clare, and moved her body so that he would enjoy it.

It really isn't making love, she thought. It's servicing a piece of equipment.

Afterwards he sat up, and he poured her more brandy in his mouthwash glass, the only one he had. He drank from the bottle.

Clare watched him closely. She was wondering when it would happen. If it would.

But he seemed contented, his body relaxed and his mind gently befuddled by the alcohol.

'It's late,' he said, more to himself. 'Too bloody late now.'

'Don't worry about it,' she said, stretching.

'Too bloody late,' he repeated.

She realized she was wrong. He didn't mean the time.

'Minus twenty-eight,' he said.

'Minus what?' said Clare.

'They think you forget the date in here,' he said. He drank from the bottle again. 'But time bloody well doesn't stand still. You know that?'

'Yes,' she said. She wanted him to go on.

He looked at her thoughtfully.

'Have you got somebody?' he said, suddenly.

She shook her head.

'Nobody? You, nobody? How come?'

'He's dead,' she said.

'Oh. I'm sorry,' he hiccuped.

He nearly said 'I'm shorry.'

He poured her more brandy.

'None of my business,' he said, 'tell me it's none of my business. You're right.'

'I don't mind,' said Clare.

'Who was he?' he asked. 'None of my business, who was he?'

'An American,' said Clare.

'Ha,' said Loach. 'Nylons from the PX, eh?'

He saw her face.

'Sorry,' he said, 'I didn't mean that. Really, I didn't.'

He was very tight.

'But he was a lucky man. I mean that. Sincerely.'

'I don't want to talk about him,' said Clare. She really didn't.

'I bet he was from Omaha,' grunted Loach. 'Was he from Omaha?'

'Let's talk about something else,' she said lightly.

'Maybe Utah. Maybe he came from Utah. That's very good,' he laughed drunkenly. 'Omaha. Utah. That's good, isn't it?'

She stared at him, fascinated.

'Utah, eh?' he insisted.

'He was from Colorado. Denver,' she said. She sensed something important.

'Denver. Pity,' said Loach and lurched against her in the bed. Some of the brandy spilt from the bottle. 'Oops,' he said.

'Got to be careful,' he said. 'Twenty-eight. That's all.'

He kissed her, but missed her mouth, he was so tight.

'Pity,' he said. 'No Omaha. No Utah. Somebody must tell them.'

She stroked his head. She was trying to stop him nodding off.

'Why twenty-eight?' she said, gently.

'Too late,' said Loach. 'Much too late. Pity.'

His eyes closed.

'Don't go to sleep,' said Clare.

'Doesn't matter,' said Loach. 'Nobody matters. I wonder who's gone instead. To tell 'em.'

'Tell them what?' said Clare very gently.

'Tell them. Omaha. Utah. Not Denver,' he was rumbling to himself.

'Why not Denver?' whispered Clare.

'Because,' said Loach and hiccuped again.

'It's wrong, is it?' she said. She was trying to make sense out of his drunkenness.

'That's right,' he said. 'The bastards wouldn't let me go. To tell 'em. Omaha beach. Utah beach. Get ready. Fuck them.'

He laughed.

'Where?' said Clare.

'Bloody beach. Not Utah at all. Not Omaha. Just code words. That's funny, isn't it? Poupeville. Grandcamp. Vierville. Nothing like bloody Utah.'

He did not seem to be conscious of her presence.

'Poupe – ville?' said Clare. She was very alert. 'Grandcamp? What's that?'

'Bloody Normandy,' said Loach. 'Cheers. We'll all see each other in Normandy.'

'You mustn't tell me this,' said Clare, urgently.

'Why not?' said Loach. 'We're prisoners. Doesn't matter. Nothing matters. Somebody's gone to tell them. Tell the circuit. Raoul Dubois brings you the landing-place. Only they wouldn't let Raoul Dubois go. Raoul Dubois is sitting here. What does it matter.'

'Normandy?' said Clare.

'Long live Normandy,' said Loach. 'Long live Utah. And Omaha. And bloody Denver.'

'When?' said Clare. She was holding on to him.

'D-day,' said Loach. 'Twenty-eight. Minus. Fuck them.'

And he fell back, dead to the world.

She gazed on him as he lay snoring. Her clothes were in a pile, but she darted round the room, naked, looking for a pencil, a scrap of paper. Loach had one in his jacket, and she tore the margin off a magazine that was lying on the bedside table.

'Omaha beach,' she wrote feverishly. 'Utah beach. Poupeville. Grandcamp.'

Desperately she tried to recall the third place. Veauville? Vienville? God, she was trained to remember things like this.

He was so drunk. Maybe she'd got it wrong ... Ah. Yes. Vierville. That was it.

And she wrote one other word:

'Normandy.'

She dressed rapidly, while Loach lay sprawled across the bed. She put the piece of paper in her bra. Then, very quietly, she left the room.

In the corridor, she thought she heard somebody. She froze in the shadows. She must not be seen. It was the middle of the night, but one never knew ...

When she got back to her room, she was soaked in perspiration.

69

In Shaw's office, Craddock took off the earphones.

The signals people had done a good job fitting microphones where they couldn't be spotted in certain rooms, and laying the wires so that nobody knew.

The sounds of lovemaking he had listened to impassively.

Then he started making notes.

Now he looked at his pad.

'Bloody hell,' said Craddock.

He picked up Shaw's scrambler line.

70

The sun was shining when Loach woke up. His mind felt heavy, and the bright light hurt his eyes. He had missed breakfast, and he would be too late for the first event of that day, a lecture about the forgery of documents which he had already sat through three times, in different forms.

The way Inverloch operated, it didn't matter whether he showed up or not. After a time, they stopped pretending.

He tried to remember exactly what had happened during the night. Clare had left nothing of her presence. Not that he expected anything. In the night, she had departed.

On the carpet, toppled over, lay the empty brandy bottle. Not that he needed it to remind himself. His mouth felt awful, his stomach floated uneasily, and his head seemed full of cotton wool.

There was no joy in him at having had Clare in his bed. Loach did not know affection. But there was satisfaction. He had wanted her. And he had had her.

The satisfaction was dimmed by the one nagging worry about what he had said. His bitterness at being in this place, his frustration at being put on ice, his fury at being stopped from carrying out his vital mission had exploded and made him do something that, once, would have been impossible.

He thought back at what he had said. Of course the memory was only vague. But he had talked. He knew that. He had mentioned the landing beaches. Or some of them. Maybe only the code names, not the actual localities. He wasn't sure. He hoped so. It was dangerous knowledge he had, and it was dangerous to pass it on.

Christ, what they had done to him. The skills of the Gestapo's best technicians could at one time not have made him reveal just some of the things he knew he had let loose in his drunken state.

He had been a good agent. He had been over there, and done well, and gone back, and done it again. He had been shrewd, and ruthless, and ever alert. And he had always known how to keep his mouth shut.

He was all right. He knew that. As long as he stayed away from women.

Suddenly, a strange thought hit him. Clare had said something about why he was here. How did she put it? 'After what you did to that girl?'

Loach's hangover evaporated in a chill. How the devil did she know? None of them here had any idea why the others had been picked for the Cooler. Sure, it was always some flaw, some weakness, some fear that had been unexpectedly revealed – but exactly what nobody was told.

Why, even the inmate himself wasn't given the reason. He might realize what it was, but they would never tell him. 'Special training' was the phrase. Or maybe, the 'you've been compromised' bit. Never the truth.

So how did Clare know?

Who had told her?

'Damn you,' said Loach.

He picked up the empty brandy bottle and threw it at the dressing-table mirror.

It smashed, and as he stared into it, his face became a grotesque mosaic.

It was the face of a man who had been betrayed.

Or had betrayed himself.

71

The clue for 17 across in the *Daily Telegraph* Crossword of 2 May had read 'One of the U.S.'. The four-letter word was 'Utah'.

It didn't worry Deception, who always did the crossword, until a day or two later, the clue for 3 down was 'Red Indian on the Missouri'. And it turned out to be 'Omaha'.

At that point, Deception's daily crossword became a high priority for him.

He had asked home security to look into it, but they were already well aware of the situation. It showed Deception how many security people do crosswords.

'It's just coincidence,' they reported to Deception.

'I don't believe in coincidence,' he said, ungraciously. 'Have you seen today's 11 across – 'But some big-wig like this has stolen some of it at times"?'

'Yes,' said one of the MI5 men, who had horn-rimmed spectacles.

'Well,' said Deception, 'it's an eight-letter word and it turns out to be "Overlord". More coincidence?'

'As a matter of fact, we've been to see them,' said the MI5 man in horn rims, 'and you'll find a clue for 11 across coming up soon that means "Mulberry", and another for 15 down reading "Neptune".'

'Just like that,' said Deception. 'All code words.'

'I'm afraid so,' said the MI5 man. 'The strangest things do happen.'

It all annoyed Deception so much that he ordered another security scrutiny of Oscar's output to check whether Grau had been up to some trickery. Deception wasn't sure how it could be tied in with crossword clues, but if there was even a hint...

They found nothing of course, and Deception decided he was allowing a slight note of frenzy to colour his day.

He went down to Bushey Park, and poured his heart out to one of Eisenhower's G-2 colonels for whom Deception had great respect.

'Don't worry about it,' said the colonel. '*Look* magazine published the whole blueprint of the North Africa invasion in November '42 three days before the landing. It happens.'

It seemed to Deception to be happening a little too much.

72

Toussaint rang Ince first thing in the morning, and said they had to have lunch that day.

'I'm sorry,' said Ince. 'There's a staff meeting in Orchard Court at 1300 and—'

'I can't talk on the phone, Major,' said Toussaint.

His voice was terse.

'All right,' said Ince. 'Where?'

'Le Petit Club,' said Toussaint.

Ince took a cab to St James's, and then walked down the little side street, and upstairs.

Toussaint was already there.

'I don't really feel hungry,' said Toussaint. 'Would you like to go in the park? It's beautiful.'

'I think I need a drink,' said Ince.

They had a glass of cheap wine each.

'I will not keep you long,' said Toussaint.

'What is it?' asked Ince.

'Let's go to the park,' said Toussaint.

Ince knew the reason. When you've got something really nasty, don't talk in a room. Don't say a word within four walls. Where there is a building, there are ears. Of one kind or another.

Talk in the open. There is nothing like a park for confiding secrets.

'Busy?' said Ince, as they crossed over into St James's.

His inbuilt suspicion of Toussaint was instinctive.

'I am going to do you a favour, Major,' said Toussaint.

'That's very good of you,' said Ince politely.

Toussaint smiled at him.

'What you really want to say to me is "Why are you doing me a favour?" '

'I expect there is a reason,' said Ince mildly.

'There is,' agreed Toussaint. 'It is, as you say, money in the bank.'

'Eh?'

'Three weeks to go before the big show, right? We may need a lot of favours from each other. Maybe you and I will be in Paris by Christmas. If I do you a favour now, perhaps you will kindly do a tit-for-tat for me?'

'I don't see how I can be much help,' said Ince cautiously.

'One day, somewhere, the moment will come,' said Toussaint. 'Meanwhile, I have a little morsel for you.'

'Oh yes?' said Ince.

'Please understand, I am not prying. This is none of my business, in one way. In another way, it is very much my affair. We are after the same thing in France. Agreed?'

'Go on,' said Ince.

'You have a girl in your Section. Very pretty. Clare Gilbert,' said Toussaint.

Ince nodded warily.

'Very attractive girl,' repeated Toussaint.

Ince stared at him.

'You know,' said Toussaint, almost as if he was changing the subject. 'One of the best agents we have across there. All the time the boche hunt him, his mother lives near Nice, at Grasse. One must take these risks, because we need people who fit ...'

The red light was starting to flash for Ince.

'Now pretty little Clare,' said Toussaint. 'She is perfect. Speaks French like a Parisienne. In fact, she is half-French, correct?'

'Go on,' said Ince.

'If we didn't use people who have next of kin under the boche, we'd be in a mess. It's a calculated risk. Like your Clare, perhaps?'

'Yes,' said Ince, dully.

'Her father is in London. Her mother is French. She was caught in the occupation.'

'She lives in Paris,' said Ince. 'Looks after her grandmother. We know that.'

'I'm afraid the grandmother is no longer alive,' said Toussaint. 'She was a very old lady, of course.'

'Mr Gilbert gets a Red Cross card from time to time,' said Ince. 'I don't think he's heard.'

'It doesn't matter,' said Toussaint. 'What I want you to know is this. The Gestapo have Madame Gilbert.'

Ince stopped dead in his tracks.

'They have her?' he said sharply.

'Some of our people have brought bad news,' said Toussaint.

'The boche know about Clare?' said Ince.

'I regret, yes,' said Toussaint. 'But it is worse. Madame Gilbert is not living in her little flat in Paris. She is staying at a villa near Fontainebleau under guard. Day and night. You see, they've got onto Clare.'

It was disaster and it came all at once.

'You sure?' said Ince quietly.

'Unfortunately, yes. Colonel Reinecke and his little AMT. They found out about Clare. They contacted her. Over here. They told her to do what they want, or her mother goes to Ravensbruck. Your Clare loves her mother ...'

'We have had no hint from Paris,' said Ince.

'Sometimes we know rather more what goes on in our own country,' said Toussaint.

'How long has she been turned?' rapped Ince.

Toussaint shrugged.

'Madame Gilbert was picked up a year ago.'

'Who's the contact here?' asked Ince.

'I do not know everything,' said Toussaint. 'What is important is that you do not rely on Miss Clare. Whatever she knows, they know.'

He left Ince soon afterwards, and made his way to Carlton House Terrace.

When Ince got back, Deception was already on the priority line.

'Listen,' he said. 'Clare Gilbert. She got the Normandy landings out of Loach. She knows where. She knows the code names. I think she's the one we're after.'

'I know,' said Ince.

73

They met hastily in the colonel's office.

'If she manages to get those names out, they know everything,' said the colonel. 'The whole thing depends on them thinking it's the Pas de Calais. That's where they are holding seven divisions in reserve. If they realize it's Normandy, and switch them ...'

'She's being watched?' asked Ince.

'Every minute and every second,' said Deception. 'Craddock is a good policeman.'

'But sooner or later she'll risk everything. Two or three minutes on the air, and phut.'

'We'll grab her now,' said the colonel. He reached for the hot phone. 'I'll tell Shaw.'

'Just a moment, sir,' said Ince.

'We haven't got any moments, Major,' said the colonel. 'She may manage to transmit any minute. God knows where she has the radio, but she must be close to it.'

'Obviously,' said Ince.

'So I'll call Inverloch now ...'

'No, sir,' said Deception.

They all swung round to him. His rank did not entitle him to tell a full colonel anything. But his tone carried the authority of a three-star general.

'I don't think we should grab her at all,' said Deception.

'Go on,' said Ince.

'I want her to get to her radio,' said Deception.

'You what!' gasped the colonel.

'And I want her to send her message.'

'Not on my authority,' said the colonel.

'Of course not,' said Deception. 'I will get my own authority.'

The colonel's buzzer went, and his secretary's voice:

'I'm sorry to interrupt, sir, but there's an urgent decode for Major Ince.'

'Excuse me,' said Ince and went out.

The colonel looked at Deception.

'You're not going to go ahead with this?' he said.

Ince came back in.

'Confirmation from Paris,' he said. 'I asked control for an urgent check on Mrs Gilbert. It's quite true her flat is empty.

The concierge says she was taken away by three men about a year ago, and hasn't been seen since.'

'So all the Red Cross cards ...'

'Fake as hell,' said Ince. 'It's her writing, but to dictation.'

'Nicely done,' said Deception. 'You must admit. We didn't have a clue. Who would bother about a middle-aged Frenchwoman whose marriage to an Englishman broke up before the war?'

'I'm sorry, gentlemen,' said the colonel. 'We're wasting time. I think we must stop this girl.'

'I think I should handle it, sir,' said Deception. 'I'll let her go ahead.'

'And what's the message she's going to send?' snorted the colonel.

'Exactly what she's found out,' said Deception. 'That it's Normandy. That we're coming ashore on beaches code named Utah and Omaha. That we're landing close by Poupeville and Grandcamp and Vierville.'

'They'd give a thousand men for that information,' said the colonel.

'Exactly,' said Deception.

74

The moment Deception came into the room, Grau knew he was in trouble.

Deception sat down, put the tips of his fingers together, and leisurely examined Grau. From head to foot. Like some peculiar specimen in the zoo.

'I think I'm going to hang you,' he said.

'That's not a very good joke,' said Grau.

'It's a pity in a way,' said Deception. 'You won't see the end of the war. You'll never find out what happens to the Fuehrer. Still, you've had a good run.'

'I've kept my bargain loyally,' said Grau.

'You mean you haven't put a foot wrong while we've been breathing down your neck, if you forgive the way I'm putting it,' said Deception.

'What else do you want me to do?' said Grau. His indigestion was starting up.

'You haven't told us a few things,' said Deception. 'We really needed to know them rather badly. But you kept quiet. Very naughty. So, another job for the hangman.'

'I've answered all your questions,' said Grau. 'You know that better than anybody.'

'I think you're rather like Goebbels,' said Deception. 'Goebbels doesn't tell many lies. He just forgets to mention some truths. I suppose he'll hang too.'

'What – what is it that I'm supposed not to have told you?' said Grau, in a low voice.

'Well now, there's quite a list,' said Deception. 'I mean, you didn't tell us that your AMT had ordered you to contact a Miss Clare Gilbert and bring her a message about her mother. When was that, Mr Harris?'

'I didn't know it – it was important,' said Grau.

'Of course not,' said Deception. 'After all, you only told the girl to hold herself available and supply your AMT with what it wants – or her mother goes into a concentration camp.'

'They were only greetings from her mother,' muttered Grau.

'Charming greetings. And you told her about Loach, didn't you? After Sylvia had been indiscreet? That's how Miss Gilbert knows what Loach had done, isn't it?'

'I never saw her again,' said Grau. 'I only brought her the original message. The rest was done ... by other means.'

'You mean, it was relayed by radio? Did you supply the radio to the girl?'

'It is very unfair of you to ask me these questions,' said Grau.

'It will be even more unfair of me to hang you after all you've done for us,' said Deception.

Grau winced. Now his indigestion hurt.

'I'm completely at your disposal,' said Grau.

'Oh, indeed you are, believe me,' said Deception.

'We are professionals,' said Grau, 'and I've no more enjoyed this than you.'

'But that's where you are so wrong,' said Deception. His grin was wolfish. 'You see, I'm enjoying every minute of it.'

'So?' said Grau. 'What now?'

'You're going to be very useful to me, or you will be very dead,' said Deception.

He flung down a *Daily Telegraph*.

'Maybe you like doing crosswords,' he snarled, and slammed the door.

75

Clare was terrified, and yet very calm.

She had to send the message now, or it might be too late.

She wondered if they had guessed anything. If Loach remembered what he had let slip, and told someone. If they had worked out that the alibi she had given for Loach was in effect an alibi for herself.

After she had killed Martin, she regretted it. It was a panic move. She realized he was security, and that he was hunting somebody. Her, in fact. But, really, there was nothing to suggest that he was on to her.

She had come down the corridor once and she thought he emerged from her room, and that worried her. Her logic told her that at Inverloch all rooms were searched from time to time, without the occupants knowing it.

But Martin was something different. One reason she had feared him was because he kept turning up in her life, as if he was on her footsteps.

So that night, when he was prowling around trying to find the radio, she had followed him. He had searched the outhouse, as if that was where one would keep such a thing.

Quickly, silently, she had crept up on him, and before he

knew quite what was happening she was twisting the garrotte round his neck, tighter, tighter ... Sadler would have been very pleased with her. It was silent killing at its best. And much more satisfying than the fight with that girl. Fighting another woman gave no great thrill. But killing a man, a slip of a girl destroying a tough, strong male ...

She hated herself for it, but she knew she had enjoyed it.

Now. She had to do it now.

She left the room. Casually. She had already processed the message. The paper was in her bra. All she needed was to get to the radio, and have a few minutes. Just a few minutes.

After that, she did not know what would happen. She was sure they would probably be monitoring the area, after her first alert message. Whether they had actually beamed in on the mansion was another matter. She had kept off the air as much as anything to prevent direction-finders beaming in on her.

She slipped along the corridor. Shaw came round the corner.

'Ah, Clare,' he said. 'How are you getting on?'

'Fine, sir,' she said.

'Excellent.'

Thank God, that was all.

But he called after her:

'Why don't you join me and Major Craddock for a drink a little later. When we're strictly off duty?'

'That would be nice,' she said.

She went into the toilet.

She locked the door. Then she stood on the cover of the bowl, and out of the cistern she lifted a case, wrapped in a watertight bag.

She opened it, and connected the radio with the light fitting. She used the lavatory chain as an aerial, and ran a wire along it. She plugged in a set of earphones. She looked at her watch. She had the piece with the coded message in one hand. The other was on the transmission key.

Quickly she tapped her call sign.

Yes, they were listening. They were on alert. Thank God.

She started tapping the message. Normandy ... Normandy ... Normandy ...

It must have been a good transmission.

The acknowledgement came at once.

She took off the earphones, rolled up the aerial wire, folded the radio back in its case, wrapped the bag round it, and replaced it in the lavatory cistern.

She didn't really care now.

76

'The chiefs of staff are very worried,' said the colonel.

'You haven't told them too much?' said Deception anxiously.

' "For their eyes only" of course,' said the colonel, 'but I did feel there was need for them to know.'

'Well, you can relax now,' said Deception.

'If reconnaissance reports that they're moving the reserves to Normandy ...' said the colonel.

'They won't,' said Deception.

Ince was watching them both.

'I thought I'd take you both to lunch,' said Deception. 'I think we can celebrate.'

'You must be joking.'

Deception rubbed his hands.

'Oscar performed very well. It was one of the longest messages, but they did tell him to take any risk necessary.'

'What did Oscar have for them?' asked Ince.

'Well,' said Deception, savouring his information, 'he sent a priority warning to Reinecke and AMT VIII. He informed them that, regretfully, Clare Gilbert had been turned by the British. That she was feeding them false information about a landing in Normandy and phoney code words about American states when obviously the invasion was coming in the Pas de Calais. That Miss Gilbert was unreliable for emotional reasons, had betrayed them and could no longer be trusted. That all her information was a plant, and that she was working for you.'

'Me,' gasped Ince.

'Yes,' said Deception. 'I thought it was a nice little bon-bon to give them your name. Who knows, they may make you an offer.'

'It's bloody risky,' said the colonel.

'Not at all,' said Deception. 'They've believed all along we're going to come across the Straits of Dover. It's the shortest and most logical route, and our friends are very logical. Normandy seems much more unlikely. Look at the map.'

'You've sentenced her mother to death,' said Ince.

'I'm afraid so,' said Deception. He was like a surgeon. 'It's unavoidable. Clare has double-crossed them.'

'But she hasn't,' said the colonel, 'it's us she betrayed.'

'Which they don't know,' said Deception. 'I do think I'm not going to hang Oscar after all.'

He stood up.

'Lunch, gentlemen?'

'I pity the girl, in a way,' said the colonel. 'She'll be lucky to get away with life.'

'Oh no,' said Deception. 'We mustn't touch her. We mustn't do anything to her. Don't you see, that will really convince them she's working for us.'

'She's a murderess,' said Ince.

'Battle training has a casualty rate of 0·5 per cent. Martin could have been hit crawling along an obstacle course. I'm sorry, Ince,' said Deception.

'It's very dirty,' said the colonel. 'The whole business is dirty.'

'Do you know of a clean one?' asked Deception.

77

On 26 June, 1944, Clare Gilbert was found dead in her room at Inverloch. She had taken an overdose of sleeping pills. She had apparently been complaining of sleepless nights, and had stock-piled the pills the medical officer gave her until she had collected a fatal dose.

78

The telegram from the War Office came to her father within twenty-four hours.

It reported that Clare Gilbert had died on active service, and expressed deep regret.

79

Ince was dictating when the phone rang.

'Yes, sir,' said Ince a couple of times. As he listened he contemplated the red crossed file in front of him.

'I have it here, sir,' he said.

The voice at the other end was very insistent.

'Quite so,' said Ince. 'I'll see to it.'

He put the phone down, and sat for a moment.

Then he said to the trim khaki-clad secretary who had been taking dictation:

'Add this. "Miss Gilbert's body has not been recovered. She is presumed drowned in the loch. In the absence of the body, there can, of course, be no post-mortem".'

The girl's pencil stopped, and she waited for more.

Ince closed the file.

'Is that all, sir?' asked the secretary.

'Yes,' said Ince, 'that's all.'